W9-AZY-613

THE LEGEND OF THE SLAIN SOLDIERS

MARCIA MULLER

THE MYSTERIOUS PRESS

Published by Warner Books

A Time Warner Company

If you purchase this book without a cover you should be aware that this book may have been stolen property and reported as "unsold and destroyed" to the publisher. In such case neither the author nor the publisher has received any payment for this "stripped book."

MYSTERIOUS PRESS EDITION

Copyright © 1985 by Marcia Muller
All rights reserved.

Cover design by Jackie Merri Meyer
Cover illustration by Phil Singer

This Mystious Press Edition is published by arrangement with the author.

The Mysterious Press name and logo are registered trademarks of Warner Books.

 Mysterious Press books are published by
Warner Books, Inc.
1271 Avenue of the Americas
New York, NY 10020

Visit our web site at
http://pathfinder.com/twep

Ⓦ A Time Warner Company

Printed in the United States of America

First Warner Books Printing: June, 1996

10 9 8 7 6 5 4 3 2 1

PRAISE FOR MARCIA MULLER
WINNER OF THE ANTHONY AWARD FOR BEST NOVEL OF THE YEAR
THE LEGEND OF THE SLAIN SOLDIERS

◇

"Exciting. . . . Spiced with fascinating information of depression-era labor struggles and the *los ranchos grandes* period of California history."
—Booklist

◇

"Tops in the increasingly crowded field of women crime writers."
—Sunday Times (Trenton)

◇

"Muller doesn't do it better just because she's been doing it longer. . . . [She] lives up to her billing as 'the founding mother of the contemporary female hard-boiled private eye.'"
—Palm Beach Post

◇

"Marcia Muller . . . quietly keeps getting better and better."
—Los Angeles Times Book Review

◇

"One can track the astounding literary growth of author Marcia Muller as she hones her skills to scalpel-sharpness."
—Cleveland Plain Dealer

◇

"Muller has gotten quietly, steadily better. She is building up steam, not running out of it."
—Newsweek

SHARON McCONE MYSTERIES
BY MARCIA MULLER

A Wild and Lonely Place
Till the Butchers Cut Him Down
Wolf in the Shadows
Pennies on a Dead Woman's Eyes
Where Echoes Live
Trophies and Dead Things
The Shape of Dread
There's Something in a Sunday
Eye of the Storm
There's Nothing to be Afraid Of
Double (with Bill Pronzini)
Leave a Message for Willie
Games to Keep the Dark Away
The Cheshire Cat's Eye
Ask the Cards a Question
Edwin of the Iron Shoes

ATTENTION:
SCHOOLS AND CORPORATIONS
MYSTERIOUS PRESS books are available at quantity discounts with bulk purchase for educational, business, or sales promotional use. For information, please write to: SPECIAL SALES DEPARTMENT, MYSTERIOUS PRESS, 1271 AVENUE OF THE AMERICAS, NEW YORK, N.Y. 10020

For Barbara Clark

One

THE TOURIST FAMILY were all eating ice-cream cones and staring at the Mayan devil figure. In the August heat the ice cream dribbled down over the cones and the tourists' fingers and then dripped onto the carpet. When one of the children put out a wet, sticky hand to touch the figurine, I started over there, my fists clenched.

Suddenly Susana Ibarra hurried past me. She gave me a wink and went up to the unlovely little family. I stopped.

"I think perhaps you would enjoy finishing your cones in our patio. It is cooler out there." She began herding them toward the large central courtyard. "And for you," she added, bending down so her face was on a level with the smallest child's, "there is a fountain into which you may put your feet!"

The tourists smiled and went docilely through the door to the patio, where water flowed merrily into the blue tiled fountain.

Susana turned to me, letting out a long sigh.

I unclenched my fists. "How do you do it?"

She shrugged, leaning against a display case that held an image of the Aztec god Xochipilli.

When I'd hired Susana to be secretary of the Museum of Mexican Arts, I hadn't expected her to become an asset. She was a giggly, gum-snapping teenager whose thieving husband had decamped to Colombia without her; I'd taken her on partly out of pity, and partly out of guilt, because I'd been responsible for his flight home. But now, two months later, she'd traded her faddish clothes for simple, colorful dresses; her long black hair flowed rather than puffing up in teased curls; and the gum was gone—at least during working hours. She still giggled enough to get on my nerves, but the giggle was part of what made her the best public-relations person we could have found. Susana's girlish manner was so disarming that she could solve the thorniest of problems and soothe the hottest of tempers. The temper she soothed most often was me.

Now she said, "I am afraid, since it is Monday, that this is only the beginning."

I nodded. "*Por Dios,* how I hate Fiesta! Thousands like them"—I motioned at the tourists who were dunking their feet in the fountain—"pouring into Santa Barbara. Parades. El Mercado. Barbecues. Mariachi bands. Drunks rioting in the bars and on the streets. Ugh!"

"Ah, but think of the money we will take in." Susana's eyes shone as she looked at the Plexiglas donation box on a stand near the entry. At three in the afternoon it was already stuffed with dollar bills from the day's visitors.

"Yes. And think of the headaches we'll have."

"Elena, you take being director too seriously. You must relax."

"How?"

"Well, what are you doing for Fiesta? Going to a party, no?"

"No. Oh, there's a barbecue and dance Saturday night at my mother's mobile-home park. I said I might stop in."

"What! At the trailer park?" Susana frowned. "Aren't they all—how do you call them—old geezers?"

I laughed. "They're pretty old."

"Well, why are you going there? What about Carlos?"

Carlos Bautista was chairman of the museum's board and my sometimes escort. "What about him?"

"Why don't you make him take you to a party? He must be invited to some fiestas *esplendidas*!"

"I don't know. He'd probably take me, but . . ."

Susana twirled a lock of hair around one finger and smiled coyly. "Elena, he is so handsome. And so *rich*!"

"He is also fifty-three years old."

"So?" She opened her eyes wide. "Take him to the trailer-park party, then. He will fit right in." She gave one of her piercing giggles.

I laughed loudly, then clapped my hand over my mouth, realizing that a serious-looking man who was about to stuff a dollar bill into the donation box was staring at me. "Come on," I said to Susana, "we have work to do." We started through the galleries to the office wing.

As we entered the folk-art gallery, with its fantastical papier-mâché animals and new, tasteful Tree of Life, Susana snapped her fingers. "Did you remember to call Jesse's grandmother?"

My mind was still on Fiesta week, and for a moment I couldn't think who Jesse was, much less his grandmother. Then I looked at the nearest *camaleon*—as the colorful animals were called—and remembered I'd promised their creator, Jesus Herrera—Jesse—that I would see his grandmother about buying a series of paintings commemorating the farm-labor movement from her.

"I can't call her; she doesn't have a phone. I'll have to drive up to Ojai to see her." Ojai was an artists' colony in the hills to the east.

"When will you go?"

"I don't know. Not today—"

One of the volunteers appeared in the door to the courtyard. Her hair was disheveled and she had ink stains all over her hands. Why, I wondered, did our volunteers always look like they were on the thin edge of desperation? For that matter, why, with the exception of Susana, did the staff? As director, I should set a better example. I should try to remain calm. . . .

"Elena," the volunteer said, "there's a phone call for you. Your mother. She says it's an emergency."

"Thanks." I quickened my pace. My mother was not one to exaggerate; if she called it an emergency, it was. When I reached the office wing, I snatched up the one on Susana's desk. "Yes, Mama."

"Elena" Her voice was shaky and subdued. "Can you come at once?"

"Mama, what is it? Are you all right?"

"Yes, yes. But you must—"

"Mama, is it Nick?" Nick Carillo was my mother's boyfriend. He was a health-food nut and jogged several miles every day, but, after all, he was seventy-eight.

"No, Elena Nick's fine. He's right here. But please come. Maybe you can help."

"I'll be there." I hung up and turned to Susana, who had been listening. "I've got to go. My mother needs me. You're in charge. Make sure somebody gets that melted ice cream out of the carpet in the pre-Hispanic gallery."

I hurried to my office for my purse, then ran out to my VW Rabbit. I stalled it twice, but finally got out of the parking lot and headed north, through the crowded festive streets to Goleta, where Leisure Village Mobile Home Park was.

Goleta is located next to Isla Vista, the site of my alma mater, the Santa Barbara branch of the University of California. From years of being late for classes, I knew all the quickest routes through town, and I arrived at Leisure Village in record time. There were police cars in the visitors' slots in the parking lot, and an ambulance was pulled up on the lawn in front of the redwood-and-glass recreation center. I parked the car at a haphazard angle and jumped out.

Over by the door to the rec center I spotted my mother and

Nick Carillo, and with them Lieutenant Dave Kirk of the Santa Barbara Homicide Squad. I hadn't seen the lieutenant since May, when the museum's director had been murdered and, as a result, I'd been promoted, but I would notice him right away in any crowd. Not that he was flamboyant-looking—quite the opposite. Kirk was brown and bland, the most nondescript, unreadable Anglo I'd ever met. Even when dealing with basics—such as last spring, when I'd thought he might be interested in asking me out—I was wrong where Kirk was concerned. I hadn't heard so much as a word from him since then.

I started over to them, then stopped. Dave Kirk? I thought. Santa Barbara Homicide? What's he doing *here*? This isn't in his jurisdiction.

And then I said out loud, "Homicide?"

Mama saw me and waved. Nick had his arm protectively around her. He was a tall, white-haired man, and my tiny, wiry mother seemed dwarfed. I hurried up to them.

"What's happened? What's wrong?"

My mother's face, remarkably smooth for a woman in her sixties, crumpled, and for a moment I thought she was going to cry. But she controlled herself—Mama never cried—and said, "It's Ciro Sisneros, Elena. Somebody murdered him."

"Oh, no!" Ciro was my mother's historian friend.

"Now, Gabriela," Nick said.

She looked up at him, her eyes narrowed fiercely. "Someone *did*."

Dave Kirk shuffled his feet and said uncomfortably, "Mrs. Oliverez, we don't know that. There's no evidence—"

"Someone *did*!" She turned to me. "Maybe you can convince him. That's why I asked you to come. You know about murder."

Dave Kirk and Nick exchanged glances.

"What are you doing here?" I said to Kirk. "This isn't your jurisdiction."

"Temporarily it is. I've been on loan to the county sheriff's department for a month now, as part of a training program. It's kept me very busy." He said the last almost apologetically, and briefly I wondered if that was why he hadn't called me.

I asked, "So why are you here if it's not a homicide?"

Again he and Nick exchanged a look. *Like mother, like daughter*, it said.

"We investigate all unusual deaths," Kirk said. "I'd think you'd know that from last spring."

"Of course." There was a commotion in the rec-center lobby. Two sheriff's men emerged and held the double doors open for the ambulance attendants. They carried a stretcher with a covered form strapped to it.

I glanced at my mother. Her eyes were full of tears and her lips trembled. She looked at me and made an effort to hold the tears back, but one spilled over anyway and she buried her face against Nick's shirt.

I felt shaken. Seeing Mama cry was like seeing one of our statues weep. But then, she'd been awfully fond of Ciro Sisneros. I'd always suspected that if Nick hadn't come along, Ciro would have eventually been her boyfriend. He was a retired professor from UC and the leading authority on local history. Over the years he'd written a whole series of books on the area—from the raising of the Spanish flag to *los ranchos grandes* to the twentieth century. The last I'd heard, he'd been working on one about Santa Barbara County during the Great Depression. I myself had liked Ciro a lot and had taken several courses from him at UC.

Now Dave Kirk touched my elbow. "Will you come with me for a few minutes?"

I nodded, glancing at Mama and then leaving her in Nick's capable hands. Kirk led me to the doors of the rec center, past a crowd of stunned-looking park residents. I nodded to Mary Jaramillo, a big woman in a Hawaiian muumuu who stood clutching one of her purebred Persian cats. She held it fiercely against her shelf of bosom, as if she were afraid death might snatch it, too. Behind her stood Sam and Gloria Walters, a happy-go-lucky couple who sometimes double-dated with my mother and Nick. Their faces were as somber as I'd ever seen them.

Kirk held the door of the rec center open and we went into its big carpeted lounge. "Dave," I said, "why does my mother keep insisting Ciro was murdered?"

He lit a cigarette and looked around for an ashtray. "She has two reasons. Both of them make it possible, although not very probable."

"My mother isn't a fanciful woman, Dave."

"I know." He finally found an ashtray on top of the baby grand piano and stuck his match in it. "And remember: I said her reasoning makes it possible—barely. Come on outside."

We went across the lounge and through the sliding glass doors to the patio. Immediately outside was an area with wrought-iron furniture and Ping-Pong tables, shaded by vine-covered latticework. Beyond that was the barbecue pit, the Olympic-size swimming pool, and the putting green. Kirk led me to the far end of the pool, near the diving board. I slowed my pace when I saw the chalk outline on the ground beside one of the raised concrete planter boxes.

"It appears to be a simple case of an old man taking bad fall and hitting the back of his head on the corner of this raised concrete." Kirk gestured at the outline with his foot. I started to speak, but he held up his hand. "I know what you're about to say—the same thing your mother did. But first, let me go over how it looks on the surface. He was here alone—"

"Where was everybody else?"

A look of irritation crossed his face, but he controlled it. I knew that in spite of the attraction between us, the lieutenant thought me a nosy woman who was all too capable of speaking and acting out of, in his opinion, "my place," but he would just have to accept me for what I was. He said, "Almost everyone from the trailer park had taken a chartered bus trip to Santa Barbara to El Mercado." El Mercado was an old-style marketplace re-created in De la Guerra Plaza every year for Fiesta week. The trip explained why Nick had been dressed in a shirt and slacks today; usually he lived in his swim trunks or jogging suit.

"Why didn't Ciro go?" I asked

"According to your mother, he was working on his current book. He saw this afternoon as a good chance to get something done without interruption. I guess this is a pretty social place, and he'd had trouble meeting his deadlines since he moved here."

That was probably true. People in the park visited back and forth a lot and were always organizing cookouts, sports events, trips, and parties. It was not a place suited to quiet contemplation.

"Anyway," Kirk went on, "Mr. Sisneros had come out and taken a swim—he was wearing a bathing suit, and a towel belonging to him was draped over one of the chairs. He probably got out of the pool, slipped, fell backward, and hit his head. Or he may have been seized by a dizzy spell. Either way, it's simple. Case closed."

"But—"

"I know. Go ahead."

"Ciro Sisneros was a very healthy man. Athletic. He jogged with Nick every morning at five-thirty. He was the judo instructor here at the rec center. He swam, miles every day. It doesn't seem likely that he would get dizzy." I pointed at the rough concrete ground. "And this is a nonskid surface. It also doesn't seem likely he would slip."

"That's exactly what your mother said." Kirk stared moodily into the bluish water of the pool. "Of course, with people in their sixties, you don't know. He could have had a heart attack or a stroke."

"Were there any of the usual signs of either?"

"No. But we won't know for certain until after the autopsy."

"Dave, what else did my mother say?"

"Huh?" The water seemed to have temporarily mesmerized him.

"You said she had two reasons for thinking it was murder."

"Yes." He turned and motioned for me to follow him. "The other, if we can find concrete evidence, would make murder more likely."

He went back through the rec center toward the front doors. I followed, glancing into the office as we passed it. The park manager, Adela Hernandez, sat at her desk talking to a uniformed deputy. For once, she wasn't wearing her usual sour expression, it having been replaced by the same slack-jawed look of shock that marked the faces of the other residents. When she saw me, she nodded solemnly, then looked back at the deputy.

The crowd outside had dispersed now that the ambulance was gone, and Mama and Nick were nowhere to be seen. I caught up with Kirk and tugged at his arm. "Dave, will you please slow down and tell me what she said?"

He turned, annoyance plain on his face again. "Your mother claims Mr. Sisneros had been threatened recently."

"By whom? With what?"

"He didn't tell her all the details. She claims he had uncovered something in the course of writing this book, something out of the ordinary. Someone else had found out about it and warned him not to research it any further or put it in the book. Mr. Sisneros was afraid—your mother had the impression he didn't know of whom. The threat was anonymous. So your mother claims."

I didn't like the way he stressed the last word. "As I said before, she's not a fanciful woman."

We started walking again, toward the cul-de-sac where both Mama's and Ciro's trailers stood. Kirk was silent, his hands clasped behind his back, his head bent.

I thought about Ciro's books. They were not scholarly tomes but entertaining and well-written accounts that brought the characters and events of local history alive in the mind of the reader. I myself had read several of them and had come away feeling I knew some of the historical figures as well as I did my own family. But they were still accounts of a long-dead past. What could Ciro possibly have discovered that posed a threat to someone in the present?

Ciro's trailer was white with a green awning extending out over the little lawn. He had planted hydrangeas in the brick-bordered flower beds, and their blue, purple, and pink blossoms covered the trailer's foundation. A uniformed officer sat on a lounge chair under the awning. He stood up when he saw Kirk and me.

Kirk nodded at him. "Elena, this is Deputy Drinnan. Deputy, Ms. Elena Oliverez."

The young man shook my hand clumsily, a puzzled look crossing his features. I didn't look official, and Kirk hadn't explained what I was doing there.

"Deputy Drinnan's been going over Mr. Sisneros's trailer," Kirk went on. To the officer he said, "Did you find anything of interest?"

The deputy took out a notepad and consulted it. I guessed he was relatively new on the force and didn't want to make any mistakes. "The deceased was very tidy and didn't have many possessions, except for books and papers. Nothing out of order in the bedroom, bathroom, or kitchen. The living room looks like he used it mainly as a study. Lots of books, most of them on history, all neatly shelved. The desk is clean, typewriter covered. There're some pages that look like a manuscript in a box next to the typewriter, but otherwise there's just the usual stuff—desk set, pens and pencils, stapler. There's a file cabinet, and everything inside is labeled by subject. No threatening notes, nothing out of the ordinary, even in his personal correspondence." He scanned the pad and then snapped it shut. "That's it, sir."

"Thank you, Drinnan," Kirk said. "We'll go inside now."

As we turned, I spied Joe Garcia, the little, somewhat seedy-looking man who lived in the next trailer. He was standing on his top step watching us, but when my eyes met his, he withdrew inside and slammed the door. Kirk glanced over there, then took my elbow and guided me up the steps into Ciro's trailer.

"Hey," he said, looking around, "this place is huge!"

I turned, smiling. "Haven't you ever been in one before?"

"No. It's like a real house."

"Yes. The term *mobile home* doesn't really apply to one of these—it's not going anywhere."

"You sure couldn't move it yourself." Kirk went up to the built-in bookcase that lined one wall. "This isn't bad. Cheaper than owning a home, I imagine."

"Quite a bit." Certainly I was aware of that. When my mother had moved here, my sister Carlota and I had bought her the trailer in exchange for the deed to the house that had always been our home. Carlota was lucky—she lived in Minneapolis, where she was a professor at the University of Minnesota, and watched her real estate appreciate from a distance. I lived in the house and called the repairman every time something broke.

Kirk took a book off the shelf and paged through it. It was Ciro's account of the days of *los ranchos grandes*—the same era that was now being honored with Fiesta.

I said, "Are you planning to go through his things?"

He reshelved the book and turned. "No. Drinnan's thorough, so that's enough of a search for now. We'll seal the place and wait for the results of the autopsy."

"And then?"

"There may be some evidence that what your mother says is true."

"Like what?"

"Bruises indicating he was pushed, for instance." Kirk picked up the manuscript box Drinnan had mentioned.

"*Poverty in Paradise: Santa Barbara County in the Great Depression.* Hmm. Looks interesting." He set it down again and ran his hand over the covered typewriter. "Let me ask you something, Elena: Are most of the people in this trailer park Chicano?"

"I'd say about three quarters. When my mother moved here, she was looking for widowers, and since she doesn't believe in interracial dating, she chose the place with the highest proportion of our own kind."

Kirk smiled. "You know, I like your mother. She's quite a woman."

"Well, Mama always knows what she wants and sets straight out to get it."

"Like her daughter."

I ignored that; from previous experience with Kirk, I knew the remark might not be as flattering as it seemed on the surface.

"Elena," he went on, "the reason I asked about the park is that sometimes, as an Anglo cop, it's difficult for me to get information out of the Chicano community. You come up here to visit your mother a lot, don't you?"

"A fair amount."

"How would you like to keep your ears open for me?"

"You mean, about Ciro?"

"Right. If you hear anything that backs up what your mother claims, here's where you can reach me." He handed me a card.

I began to grin. I couldn't help it. The grin spread over my face, and as it did, a frown spread over Kirk's. I said, "You're going to listen to me this time, eh?"

"Now, Elena—"

"No more ridiculing my theories? No more ignoring my suggestions?"

"I've already admitted I was wrong about Frank De Palma's murder." Frank De Palma was the former director of the museum.

"You certainly were."

"I said I've admitted that—several times, and humbly."

I decided to be gracious and back off. "Okay, Dave, I'll let you know anything I hear." I dropped the card in my purse and turned to go. It was time to check on how Mama was doing.

Two

I FOUND MAMA sitting on the couch in the living room of her trailer. Her eyes were dry now, but she stared into space, her work-worn hands clasped in her lap. Her feet barely touched the floor, and she looked so tiny and forlorn that I felt a sudden rush of protective feeling toward her. After all, Ciro's death had been a terrible shock, and Mama was no longer young. Sometimes I forgot that because she was so energetic and vital.

Nick came out of the little kitchen, carrying a coffeepot and cups on a tray. He set it down on the table and began to pour. Mama looked around as if she'd just realized we were there. Then she sat up straighter and pinned back a lock of long gray hair that had escaped the barrette at the nape of her neck.

"So, Elena," she said, "what did the lieutenant tell you?"

"A few interesting things." I took a cup of coffee from Nick's outstretched hand and sat down. "He's not as sure about Ciro's death being an accident as he'd like to seem."

Mama's eyes flashed and she looked at Nick. "You see?"

Nick sat down next to her. "Yes, Gabriela, I see." His voice was weary, and I glanced anxiously at him. Nick, like my mother, was not a person I thought of as being old or tired.

"What did Lieutenant Kirk say that makes you think that?" Mama asked me.

"It's more what he didn't say."

"Oh." She looked disappointed.

"Anyway," I went on, "Kirk says he'll know more after the autopsy. It will at least show if Ciro fell because he had a stroke or a heart attack, or if he might have been pushed."

"Of course he was pushed!" Mama said. "Didn't I tell that lieutenant that someone had threatened Ciro—"

"Gabriela," Nick said, "drink your coffee."

She did, and I followed suit. It was awful—too strong and full of chicory. I set the cup down on the table and went to the refrigerator for some wine. Nick frowned when he saw it and looked at his watch. Nick was a health nut, and some of the most spirited discussions we'd had were over my care— or lack thereof—of my body.

"Anyway," I said, hoping to forestall one of those debates, "Dave Kirk wants me to keep my ears open when I'm up here."

"For what?" Nick asked.

"Anything related to Ciro. You two can do the same—I'll deputize you." I smiled, trying to lighten the atmosphere, but they didn't respond. "Mama, tell me more about this threat Ciro received."

She set her coffee cup down. "He said someone didn't want him to go on with his research for the book about the Depression. He didn't know who, but he suspected why, and it made him afraid."

"Did he explain why? I mean, the reason he suspected?"

"No."

"How was he threatened? A letter? A phone call?"

"Someone telephoned. He didn't recognize the voice."

"Was it male or female?"

"He couldn't tell. It was muffled."

"And what did this person say?"

Mama sighed. "Ciro didn't repeat the exact words. Now I wish I'd asked him. All he said was he had been told to stop working on the book or else."

"Or else?"

"Just that. Or else."

"Was he going to? Stop, I mean."

"No, of course not. That to Ciro would have been like stopping breathing." Mama paused, listening to the echo of her words, then crossed herself. "What I mean is, Ciro's work was his life. He said that sometimes there was danger, even in historical research, but that he'd have to accept that danger. He said he had an obligation to the truth."

"The truth about what?"

"I think he meant truth, you know, as a general principle."

I stood up and got more wine. This time Nick pushed his lips out belligerently. It made him look a little like a bulldog.

"Tell me about Ciro," I said to my mother.

"He was a fine man. A very fine man."

Nick shot her a glance, and his face became even more jowly. *Por Dios,* I thought, he's jealous of a dead man.

"What about his background?" I asked. "Who were his people?"

"His great-grandfather was a don, a *soldado distinguido.* He was granted that huge tract of land down the coast—Topanga Malibu Sequit. Of course, they eventually lost it, but once most of Malibu Beach and Topanga Canyon belonged to the Tapia family."

During the Spanish rule in Alta California—from 1822 through the gold rush—a much-romanticized life-style had developed. The Spanish government had deeded large ranchos to its distinguished soldiers, and there these veterans lived with seemingly effortless grace and charm—an indolent elegance that masked the grueling manual labor, usually performed by Indians and low-class colonists from Mexico, that was required to run the large cattle spreads. With the American takeover, many of the ranchos had been confiscated or overrun by squatters. Other families, because of the dons' inordinate fondness for horse-racing and gambling, ran up huge debts that forced them to take on heavy mortgages or sell off parcels of their land. The era of *los ranchos grandes* had lasted little more than thirty years, but it is responsible for many of the Spanish-based traditions of southern California. I considered some of these traditions, such as Fiesta week, to be major commercialized annoyances, designed to give lovers of tranquility such as me one whopping big headache.

I said, "Ciro was a Tapia, then?"

"On his mother's side. She married beneath her, the family thought—but the young man was smart and did well in business, in spite of not having much in the way of background. At least, he was able to send Ciro to Stanford."

"Stanford? With all those rich Anglos?"

"Yes. I gather it wasn't a completely pleasant experience. He often said it made him into a loner, which is one reason he never married."

"I can imagine it would have had that effect." I remembered my own days at UCSB. It was a very different type of school from Stanford, and of course by then things had changed a great deal since Ciro's college days. But all the same, there had been little distinctions I'd been aware of, such as the sororities that didn't take Chicanas; and the wealth of my Anglo classmates who didn't have to work, while I often came to lectures with my hair still smelling of grease from the drive-in where I served hamburgers part-time.

"Anyway," Mama said, "Ciro built a very distinguished career. And he also used to say that if he had married and had a family, he might never have written his books."

"Probably not." The way things were with my job, I couldn't imagine having a husband and children—and I wasn't trying to write books on top of it. We were silent for a minute, and then I said, "I wish I'd asked Dave Kirk if I could take Ciro's manuscript of the Depression book from his trailer."

"Why?" Nick asked.

"There might be something in it that would point out why

somebody would have threatened him. The trailer's sealed, though. I can probably get Kirk to let me in there, but I doubt I'll be able to reach him until tomorrow."

"You don't have to wait for him." Mama got up and went to the little desk on the opposite wall. "I happen to have a copy of the manuscript."

"What are you doing with it?"

"Ciro always Xeroxed his day's work and left it with me for safekeeping. He thought it was a risk to have only one copy."

"Why?"

"Well, what if his trailer caught fire and he wasn't home to save it?"

Nick snorted loudly. I looked at him in surprise.

"The real reason," he said to me, "was that Ciro wanted to come over here and flirt with your mother."

"Now, Nick." Mama handed me a thick manila envelope.

"Well, it's true. Anyone could see that."

Mama's eyes began to sparkle a little. "Ciro and I had a purely intellectual relationship."

"That doesn't mean he didn't have his hopes."

"Regardless of his hopes, my feelings for him were strictly platonic."

"Huh. I'll bet. He *was* fifteen years younger than me. Next to Ciro, I probably looked like an old fogey."

"Of course. But I *like* old fogeys."

"Now just a minute, Gabriela—"

I gathered up the manuscript and my purse and left them to bicker. It was one of their favorite pastimes and sure to cheer them both up.

When I got back to the museum, things were winding down for the day. The visitors and most of the volunteers had left, except for Emily Hitchens, who was manning the little gift shop in the main entry. Emily was an Angla—a young woman with ash-blond hair, pretty in a wispy, insubstantial way. She'd come to us two weeks before, wanting to volunteer, and since then she'd quietly gone about whatever job was handed to her, speaking only when spoken to, being cheerful and polite but making no friends. She interested me because of her obvious reluctance to let anyone get too close to her. Now I went up to where she stood behind the counter, polishing a replica of a pre-Hispanic figurine.

"How has your day gone?" I asked.

"Very well. We sold the usual assortment of postcards and calendars—plus one of those big lacquerware platters."

"That's a relief. When we decided to stock them, I wasn't sure such an expensive item would sell." I paused. "How are you enjoying your work here, Emily?"

She straightened a pile of books on contemporary pottery, aligning their edges with that of the counter. "Very much. It's interesting."

"We should have coffee sometime soon. There really hasn't been a chance to get to know one another."

"Yes." She clasped her hands together, and I had the feeling she was trying to keep them from trembling.

"Why don't you stop by my office tomorrow morning? I'll send Susana out for doughnuts, and we can talk."

"Fine." She smiled mechanically and then looked down at her hands.

I crossed the central courtyard to the office wing, pondering Emily's strange response to a simple invitation to coffee. She'd acted almost afraid of me. Me, whom I consider to be the world's least intimidating individual. There was something odd about that woman, and right then I decided to get to the bottom of it. We'd had trouble in the past with employees and volunteers who harbored secrets, and I didn't want it happening again.

The office wing was quiet in the late-afternoon heat, the phones and the rattle of typewriters stilled. Susana's desk was cleared, the chair pushed into the kneehole. I frowned, wondering if she'd gone home early. I'd left her in charge—

And it seemed she had taken me literally. When I went into my office, I found her sitting in my padded leather chair, her head bowed over an art book that I identified by the color plate of a twentieth-century devil fantasy figure as one from my own bookshelf.

"Trying the chair out for size?" I spoke tartly because it hadn't been my chair for long and I didn't like to see anyone usurp it, however temporarily.

Susana started and looked up, her face coloring slightly. "Elena, I didn't hear you come in! The emergency—is that all taken care of?"

"More or less."

Susana stood, shutting the book and returning it to the shelf under the window. "It was not too serious, I hope."

"It was serious, but there was nothing I could do about it." I set my purse and Ciro's manuscript down on the desk.

Susana edged toward the door. "I came in here to study."

"To study what?"

"Your art books. I have been borrowing them when I have nothing to do. After all, if I am to work here, surely I should know something about the collections."

"Of course. It's perfectly all right to read them, as long as you remember to put them back—and don't crack the spines."

She smiled, her initial confusion gone. "Is it all right if I leave now, Elena? I have many errands to perform on the way home."

"Certainly. I'll lock up when it's time. Have a nice evening."

She went out, and I sat down in the chair, still annoyed at having seen her there. Why? I asked myself. Susana was only the museum secretary; *I* was director. Susana had a year of junior college behind her; I had an art-history degree from UCSB. What possible threat could her sitting in my chair pose? Just because she'd mastered her job so well and quickly didn't mean she intended to go after mine next.

But then I remembered a different side to Susana I'd once seen—a cold and cruelly calculating one.

Stop being insecure, I told myself. Stop worrying about Susana, and start reading Ciro's manuscript.

I pulled the pages from the manila envelope. They were neatly typed, with only occasional corrections made in felt-tip pen. Leaning my elbows on the desk, I began reading.

Ciro opened by describing the land around Santa Barbara as it had been in the thirties—a more open, agricultural land, free of the shopping centers and housing tracts that now threatened to spoil it. But even back then, in the eyes of the longtime residents, something had loomed ugly against the scenery: the makeshift camps of the people who had left their poverty-stricken homes and come to southern California with the hope that there might be a livelihood here.

What they had found, however, could scarcely be called a livelihood. There was work, yes—exhausting toil in the fields from sunup to sundown, for a pittance. But it wasn't steady work, and when their long day was done, that pittance—all of it—went for food that did not nourish, for shelter that did not keep them warm and dry. They looked around at the people who owned the land, the people who had the things they lacked, and they wanted a share of it.

The people who *had* could see the hunger in the eyes of the have-nots, and it made them afraid. And so they lashed out with rougher treatment of their hired laborers, restrictive laws, even brutality—

The phone rang. I glared at it, hoping someone else would answer. It rang twice more, the first button flashing, and I realized I was probably the only one left in the office wing. Snatching up the receiver, I said, "Museum of Mexican Arts."

"Elena?" It was the deep voice of our board chairman, Carlos Bautista.

"Yes, Carlos. How are you?"

"Fine, fine. Where is your secretary, that you're answering your own phone?"

"I sent her home early." Glancing at my watch, I noted that soon everyone else would be going and I would have to lock up.

"Such a kind boss, you are, Elena! I wish I had one who was so good to me."

I laughed. Carlos was his own boss, a man who early in life had made a fortune in oil. "I guess the boss is always hardest on himself."

"That's true. Tell me, are you busy this evening?"

I hesitated, looking down at Ciro's manuscript. "I have a lot to do."

"Let it go for now and come to a party with me. My friends, the Rodriguezes—you know them, they own La Corona Winery in the Santa Ynez Valley—are giving a dinner in honor of some houseguests who are here for Fiesta I can guarantee that the fine wines will flow."

"Oh, Carlos, it'll be a fancy party, and I haven't anything to wear." He was always inviting me to parties thrown by his rich friends—gatherings I found intimidating and boring at the same time.

"Nonsense. What about that dress you wore to the Cinco de Mayo party? The white one?"

"I can't wear that. It looks like a *vestido de boda*."

"So what's wrong with looking like a bride? Someday, you know—"

"Carlos, I really have a lot to do tonight."

"Elena, please, put on the wedding dress and come with me."

"Well. . ." Again I looked down at the manuscript. Recently I'd turned into a night owl for some reason; I could always read it later, after the dinner party. And Susana had been right this afternoon: I should get out more. "All right."

"Good. I will call for you at seven."

I hung up the phone. That gave me only two hours to get presentable enough for a formal party at a winery. Short notice—which meant Carlos had probably had another date who canceled at the last moment.

Oh well, I thought philosophically, so what if I'm not first in his affections? He's certainly not first in mine.

What I really needed was a younger boyfriend, someone I could share my interests and friends with. But I wasn't going to find him by sitting around the house and reading a history manuscript. Maybe there would be someone interesting and under age fifty at the party; and if not, at least—as Carlos had promised—the fine wines would flow.

Three

WHEN CARLOS ARRIVED to pick me up, I was standing at my front window looking at the obstacle course the neighbors' children had left on the sidewalk. Composed of bicycles and tricycles, skates and balls, it was as effective as a rat's maze—and far more dangerous. I'd have to complain to the parents before somebody, particularly one of the older residents, tripped over it and was hurt. It didn't bother me to have to complain, though; the neighbors had done the same about *my* obstacle courses years ago, and, like my mother, the parents of these kids wouldn't resent it.

Carlos got out of his black Cadillac Seville and locked the door, then turned and surveyed my house. His tanned face wore the expression of dismay it always did when confronted with my California bungalow, and I knew he was mentally cataloging the scraggly lawn, faded green paint, missing roof tiles, and—the latest disaster—the broken trellis that allowed the giant fuchsia bush to trail all over the porch. I was sure that Carlos occasionally entertained ideas about taking me away from all this, and it annoyed me because I didn't want to be taken anywhere. True, the place needed fixing up, but I'd already contacted the roofer and had almost enough money saved for the paint job. And if I ever could take some time off from the museum, I knew I could shore up trellises and sow grass seed as well as anyone.

Carlos started up the walk. He was a big, well-built man

with wavy iron-gray hair, handsome in a rugged way. Tonight he looked especially well turned out in a light summer suit, and, watching the way he carefully avoided stepping on the trailing fuchsia blossoms, I felt a surge of affection for him. After all, Carlos couldn't be blamed for his dismay at my surroundings; a widower, he had a graceful Spanish-style home up in the hills in the area called the Riviera. My stucco bungalow in the flatlands must have presented quite a contrast.

The living room was strewn with newspapers and art journals, and I didn't want to inflict this less obvious flaw on him, so I picked up my purse and stepped out onto the porch.

"Elena," Carlos said, taking my hand in his courtly way, "you look lovely."

"Thank you. But I do hope your friends won't think we've come directly from the wedding chapel."

"If they did, it would only flatter me." He led me to the car and, as he handed me in, planted a chaste kiss on my cheek. I glanced across the street and saw Mrs. Nunez watching from her porch. She was the nosiest old lady on the block and watched the progress of my life with great interest. I smiled, thinking how surprised she would be to know a kiss was all I ever got from Carlos. He was old-fashioned and as conscious of the twenty-five-years difference in our ages as I was. The combination did not permit much in the way of intimacies.

Chatting about the museum and occasionally lapsing into comfortable silence, we drove out of town and over San Marcos Pass to the Santa Ynez Valley, some forty miles to the northeast. The sun was sinking behind us, and at first it bathed the hills in fiery light, then cast purple shadows as we dropped down into the valley. The land here was still much as Ciro had described it in the introduction to his manuscript— softly rounded hills interspersed with fields of multicolored flowers and flat cattle range. We followed the main road, which was once the stagecoach route north, then turned off onto a side route. Vineyards began to appear, rows of grape plants stretching to the hills beyond.

While wine-making in the Santa Barbara area had begun in the late 1700s with the Franciscan friars, most of the vineyards we were passing through were relatively new. Close to ninety percent of the commercial grape acreage had been planted since 1971, and the fledgling wineries were already doing well, their recent vintages taking prizes in wine competitions and attracting positive critical attention. La Corona Winery, I knew, produced an excellent Cabernet Sauvignon; the grape for this popular wine thrived on the climate here, which was tempered by afternoon ocean breezes.

After a few miles Carlos slowed the car and turned through an ornate stone-and-iron gate. The driveway, bordered by a low stone wall, cut a straight line through more acres of grapevines and ended in a circular parking area in front of a massive fieldstone house. A number of expensive cars were parked there, and already I began to feel sorry I had agreed to come.

Sounds of voices came from within as we went up to the front door, which was flanked by two large sculptures of lions. Carlos rang the bell, reaching out to pat the head of the nearest beast with easy familiarity. The door was opened by a dark-suited, extremely correct man—the British butler whom Carlos had mentioned the Rodriguezes had recently hired—but before he could announce us or do whatever else butlers were supposed to, we were pounced upon by a cloud of turquoise silk. Alicia Rodriguez, clad in a voluminous caftan embroidered in gold-and-pink thread. The hostess had never been one to stand on ceremony.

The butler withdrew—concealing, I was sure, what would have been a very unbutlerly frown—and Alicia dragged us through the entry and into a large room overlooking a terrace. There were at least twenty people there, milling about with wineglasses in hand. A maid in a dark uniform passed us with a tray, and Alicia plucked glasses off it and extended them to us.

"I'm so glad Carlos brought you," she said to me. "How are you? How are things at the museum? What a lovely dress! Where did you get it? It's so traditional; I love traditional things."

I looked around for Carlos. He was being buttonholed by Dean Montross, one of the men who was involved in an oil-drilling venture with him.

"Elena, you must meet my friend Diane." Alicia was pulling me toward the terrace door. "This party's in honor of her and her husband Bob. They're visiting from the San Joaquin Valley, for Fiesta."

The woman she introduced me to was classically beautiful, with pale blond hair rolled into an old-fashioned French knot. I stared at the necklace she wore, strands of delicate seed pearls interspersed with lapis lazuli beads. Her long silk dress was the exact shade of the lapis, and its style was understated, presumably to call attention to the necklace. As Alicia introduced us, I suddenly felt as if I were eight years old and had just come in from making mudpies.

"Elena is director of the Museum of Mexican Arts in Santa Barbara," Alicia said. "She's doing such a wonderful job— oh, there's Ronny. I must greet him and tell him how much I liked his latest film. . . ." And then she was off, in a whirl of turquoise.

I looked around again for Carlos. He was a couple of yards away, deep in conversation with Dean Montross. I caught the words "offshore drilling" and decided I'd better not join them. The last time I'd been in on a discussion of offshore drilling with Carlos and his cronies, I'd made a caustic remark, something along the lines of "One spill out there in the channel and you'll have a lot of dead birds and fish on your hands again." They'd looked at me as if I were demented and then politely gone on talking. No, I was better off here, with the beautiful Diane.

Diane, I found, was studying me with wide baby-blue eyes. "The Museum of Mexican Arts," she said. "Isn't that the place where the director was murdered last spring?"

"Yes. Fortunately, the killer was caught. And the museum is now operating normally."

"And you were given the director's job?"

"Yes. Before, I was curator. Actually I still am; we haven't found anyone to replace me yet."

"You must know a lot about interior decorating."

The leap in logic it must have taken to bring her to that conclusion startled me. "Um . . ."

"Alicia and I just got back from a big decorating show in San Francisco. At the Ice House. We try to go up there a couple of times a year to look at the new furniture."

"I see."

"The new styles are really very impressive." She sounded as if she was quoting from a manufacturer's brochure. "Basic beige is out; gray is in. Violet grays. Blue-green grays."

"It sounds . . . lovely."

"They're using new materials, too."

"Oh?"

"Stone."

"Stone?"

"Stone." She nodded solemnly, then took my hand and led me back inside, to a corner of the entryway. "Look what Alicia bought."

I looked. It was a chair—or at least I thought it might be one. Carved of what looked like polished granite, it had a high slanted back and raised arms. Supporting each of the arms was a creature with a long snout, curved talons, and folded wings.

"What . . .?" I said.

"Griffins. They're very popular this year."

"Griffins." It was enough to make one's head spin. Immediately I thought of Jesse Herrera's papier-mâché animals. Perhaps I should advise him to start turning them into chairs. Of course, he'd have to work with sturdier materials . . . .

"Elena, there you are." Carlos had come up behind me. "Hello, Diane. Alicia sent me to escort you two ladies. It seems we're all to share a table for dinner."

Oh, lovely, I thought. Maybe Diane can tell us all about the latest trend in sofas. A nice stone sofa, supported at each corner by a brontosaurus. . . .

But I allowed Carlos to take me on his arm and escort me to the terrace, where round tables, each set for six, were arranged. He seated Diane and me, and then we were joined by her husband, Bob, a beefy fellow who looked like an outdoorsman—and indeed was a rancher in the San Joaquin Valley, according to Carlos. A few minutes later, Alicia arrived in a swirl of silk that almost obscured Ramon, her slender, unobtrusive husband. Prawns sauteed in a garlic sauce were placed in front of us, and then, *Dios Gracias,* the wine began to flow as promised.

Initially, the talk centered around "the girls'" trip to San Francisco, then went into a discussion of future Fiesta week doings—parties that I certainly hadn't been asked to attend. I said little, looking around at the people at the other tables. They were all in their forties and fifties, all well dressed and affluent-looking. And most of them were Anglos. It didn't surprise me; I'd long ago realized that when one becomes as rich as Carlos or the Rodriguezes, one forms alliances with other rich people, rather than along ethnic lines. These Anglos accepted Carlos and Alicia and Ramon because of their wealth and—in a manner they probably considered extremely tolerant—overlooked their Hispanic origins. They accepted me primarily because Carlos had brought me, but also because I was in the arts field and therefore practically a conversation piece.

It made me uncomfortable to be in a situation where I wasn't simply taken at face value—indeed, where my being a Chicana was something to be ignored or even forgiven. In the last couple of years I'd come to identify more and more with my heritage and my own people. It hadn't always been that way—I'd had more than my share of Anglo friends and a penchant for Anglo boyfriends—but recently that was changing. Maybe it was working at the museum; maybe it was simply coming of age. But whatever the reason, it made me feel definitely out of place here. I didn't stop the waiter when he refilled my wineglass a third and then a fourth time.

After a while, the talk turned to Diane and Bob's ranch in the valley, where they grew lettuce. Bob was worried about his profit margin, citing the case of a large Salinas Valley grower who had shut down because lettuce was no longer profitable.

"You've got your low produce prices, coupled with high labor costs," he said. "Frankly I don't know how much longer small growers like me can stay in business."

I thought his profit margin must be pretty substantial, judging from all those lapis and pearls hanging around his wife's neck, but I merely picked at my entrée and took a big swallow of wine.

"That Salinas grower," Ramon said, "wasn't there some stink about the shutdown—something having to do with a contract he'd just signed with the United Farm Workers?"

"Yeah. It put eight hundred field workers out of a job, but what can you do? The union, of course, claims the shutdown was a ruse to reopen without a union."

"Was it?" I asked.

Everyone looked surprised, because I'd been so silent up until now. Ramon shrugged. *"Quien sabe?"*

I found it interesting that he slipped into our native tongue only when speaking to me.

"I've heard of a lot of incidents like that," Carlos said.

"Didn't one of your melon packers over in the valley recently refuse to renew a UFW contract?"

"Actually, it was the workers. The packer was calling for a ten-percent pay cut, and the union wouldn't go for it. They went out on strike, and the packer brought in nonunion workers who were willing to hire on at half the union wage. They can do that now, with the high rate of unemployment. People who have been out of work for a long time will take anything they can get."

"It looks to me," Ramon said, "like the unions are running scared."

"They're on the defensive, that's for sure."

The waiter took the plates away and began serving dessert.

"Of course," Carlos said, "what this is going to do is produce a potentially dangerous situation. Didn't you have riots in the valley, Bob?"

"Yeah. We had a chief of police knocked unconscious by a mob. One crowd armed itself with fence posts that had been sharpened like spears, for God's sake. There's the usual stuff: beatings of nonunion workers, smashed windshields, pickets getting pelted by rocks or almost run over. And then there was the Dominguez murder case."

"I hadn't heard about that," Carlos said.

"It was three months ago, up around Visalia. Labor organizer by the name of Tomas Dominguez got into a fight with one of the growers' foremen. Beat him up pretty badly, then came back that night and shot him dead. Dominguez ran; by now he's probably deep into Mexico. The killing was senseless. The whole labor movement's senseless."

I looked down at my dessert plate, which held pink sherbet frozen into a perfect rose. The rose had six green leaves positioned around it, and they were already beginning to run.

"I guess it wouldn't seem so senseless to you if *you* had lost your livelihood," I said.

They all looked at me again with that expression of mild surprise.

"What do you mean, Elena?" Carlos said.

"I mean those *campesinos* on the picket lines—fighting for the right to make a living isn't exactly senseless."

"They were given the chance to make a living," Bob explained gently, as if I were Indeed the eight-year-old I'd felt like earlier. "They were merely asked to take a pay cut so their employer could maintain his profit margin."

I toyed with my dessert spoon, then set it down. "I don't think the word 'merely' applies to the situation."

"I don't understand."

"Do you know what the average *campesino* makes?"

"It can run up to twelve-fifty an hour."

"But it's more likely to be six- to seven-fifty. That's not a lot of money, and when you take ten percent off the top—"

"It's damned good money for unskilled labor. Why, most of those people own their homes, have cars and TVs—"

"Most of 'those people' hang on marginally. You take ten percent off their pay and it will cause their lives to collapse."

There was silence for a moment. I stared down at the pink sherbet petals, which were mingling with the green to produce an almost gray color. Gray-green, which was very popular this year.

Alicia, always the saver of awkward situations, spoke. "Elena's right, you know. And I think it's good she's concerned about her people. All of us would do well to have more of that concern."

My people. Not hers, in spite of having one hundred percent Mexican blood.

"And the unions are doing wonderful things," she went on. "The adversity may actually be just what they need to revive their spirit. In recent years they've become moribund. Where did I read something about that? *Time? Newsweek?*"

Of course everyone waited breathlessly while she pondered.

Most of the breathlessness was due to the fear that her pause might give me the opportunity to speak again.

"It must have been *Time*. There was a story on how they have revived the Fiesta of the Slain Soldiers."

"The what?" Bob asked.

"Fiesta of the Slain Soldiers." Then she added with a glance at me, *"Fiesta de los Soldados Muertos.* It started back in the Depression, something to do with some labor leaders who were murdered. In the early days of *La Rosa* it was a big event, but for a while now they haven't held it."

"When does this event occur?" Carlos asked.

"Right about now, roughly the same time as our Fiesta."

Diane spoke for the first time since the conversation had turned from parties and interior decorating. "Where is it held? Can we go?" Obviously, she saw it as an occasion that might call for a new dress.

Alicia smiled, but not without a trace of irritation. "I don't think you'd enjoy it, Di. It's held all over, in the barrios and migrant labor camps."

"Oh." Diane looked off at the far side of the terrace, where a band was setting up.

Alicia took this as the opportunity to end the meal. Rising, she said, "Let's allow the waiters to clear so we can enjoy the dancing."

Everyone got up but Carlos and me. I glanced down at my plate once more. The rose was a blob of pink, encircled by fashionable gray-green.

"Elena," Carlos said, "don't you feel well?"

I didn't feel well at all, but not in the way he thought, and I couldn't explain it—not to Carlos. So I merely told him something he'd understand: "No, I'm sorry, but for some reason I have a terrible headache."

He nodded sympathetically, and we left a short while later, making our thanks to our most gracious host and hostess.

Four

When I opened the museum the next morning, the sun was shining in a lightly cloud-dusted sky. It promised to be a fine summer day, and as I turned on the little fountain in the courtyard and stood watching the light play on its water, I realized my bad feelings from the night before had faded.

I waved to Susana, who was just arriving, and went into my office. Plunking down the big canvas tote bag I carried, I took out Ciro's manuscript and set it to one side on the desk. After going home last night, I'd begun reading it again and had gotten through the chapter about the WPA projects—Santa Barbara had realized such notable improvements as having the city dump turned into a baseball field—before I'd fallen asleep on the couch. Perhaps today there would be an opportunity to read further.

But first I decided to check on how the special exhibit for Fiesta had turned out. Although we hadn't yet found a new curator, I'd arranged to have two volunteers come in from the art-history department at the university, and they had put together a display of paintings, ceramics, and crafts dating from the era of *los ranchos grandes*. Since these were all by Hispanic or Indian citizens of Alta California, rather than Mexicans, I was violating the principle under which the museum had been founded, but we had already done that by exhibiting the work of local Chicano artists, such as Jesse Herrera. It was a direction in which I was determined to take the museum; as an institution largely supported by Santa Barbarans, it ought to reflect the present composition of the community as well as its Mexican heritage.

I crossed the courtyard again, smiling at a pair of visitors who were just arriving, and went into the little gallery reserved for special exhibits. When we'd inherited the old adobe from a deceased board member last spring, this space had been a junk room, but I'd seen its possibilities and had had it cleaned and fixed up in time for Fiesta. The volunteers had been just applying the final touches when I'd locked up last night, and I hadn't had time to really scrutinize the display, but now I saw that they had done an excellent job on it. There was a grouping of oils depicting the *ranchos,* including a magnificent *vaquero* on his horse, which was particularly impressive. And the religious triad—the Mission, a blessing by a padre, and a vineyard with the bell tower in the background—was emotionally powerful.

The inspection completed, I returned to my office in time for a meeting with our accountant. After certain events last spring, I'd decided that calling in an outside bookkeeping service was the way to handle the museum's accounts. And I was more than pleased with Keith Sullivan, the man they'd assigned to us. He was a diminutive redhead with a thick Irish brogue, and he credited me with having the intelligence to understand what he was doing with the accounts. Once every week he would appear with his battered briefcase and go over the figures with me. Keith was an enthusiastic accountant, and he would mumble and exclaim and show me equations he'd worked out on his calculator. Unfortunately, I couldn't understand him half of the time, and after a month I had realized that most of the mumblings and exclamations were for his own pleasure, not my edification. Since then I'd stopped straining my ears, and merely nodded and smiled to show how clever I thought he was. And since we could always pay the lighting bill these days, I decided that Keith was doing his job.

When he finally left, I looked at my calendar, saw I had no appointments, and reached for Ciro's manuscript. I turned to chapter five, and someone spoke my name from the doorway. Looking up in annoyance, I saw Emily Hitchens standing there, her hands clasped primly in front of her.

"You wanted to see me this morning," she said.

Por Dios, I'd forgotten all about it and hadn't had time to plan what approach I would take with this very strange volunteer. "Yes, Emily," I said, setting the manuscript aside. "Come in and sit down." Then I pressed the button on the intercom and asked Susana to take some money from petty cash and get us all doughnuts to go with our coffee.

Emily sat across the desk from me, smoothing her beige skirt over her knees. Sunlight from the little barred windows shone on her, and her face, framed by limp wings of her fine pale hair, looked bloodless. I wondered if she might be in poor health.

"So," I said, "tell me about yourself."

She hesitated, running the tip of her tongue over her lips. "There's not much to tell."

"Are you from Santa Barbara?"

"No."

"Oh? Where, then?"

"A little town near Fresno called Lindsay."

"Where the olives come from." Lindsay was an agricultural town, best known for that fruit.

She smiled tentatively. "Yes."

"Did you grow up there?"

"Yes."

"I suppose your folks grew olives."

"No, citrus fruit. It was a small ranch, and we all had to pitch in." A reminiscent light came into her gray eyes, and for a moment she seemed more alive. "On cold mornings my brothers and I would have to tend the smudge pots. It wasn't considered girls' work, but I only had two brothers, and you have to move fast when there's frost. I took a lot of ribbing for being the only girl in my homeroom to have a permanent excuse because of smudging."

I laughed softly. "Did you come straight to Santa Barbara from Lindsay?"

"No." The light went out of her eyes, and she lowered her gaze to her hands. "I . . . I bummed around for a while."

She didn't look like the kind of young woman who would "bum around," but I let it go for now. "And your interest in art—how did you develop that?"

"Oh . . . I guess I've always had it."

"In Mexican art specifically, or in all types?"

"All types. When I came here, I read in the paper that this museum was looking, for volunteers, and it seemed a good place to learn. . . ."

I waited, but she didn't complete the thought. "You've certainly helped us a lot since you've been here. In fact, you've worked almost full-time. Do you also have a job?"

"Um . . . no. I mean, I have some money saved, and I thought I could learn something."

"Did you ever think of working for the museum? For pay, that is?"

She shrugged.

"The reason I ask is that the museum is growing. If you were to decide what type of work you like and perhaps get some training—"

Susana appeared in the doorway with two cups of coffee and a box of doughnuts. She set the cups down and let us both make our selections from the box. Then she took her shorthand pad from where it was tucked under her arm and said, "I am sorry to interrupt you like this, but we must go over your schedule, Elena."

"Schedule? What schedule?"

"There is a great deal to be done. For one thing, the Fiesta float."

"For the parade? I thought we'd decided not to have one. It's too expensive."

"Mr. Bowman"—he was a wealthy Anglo contributor—"has offered to donate the money. Jesse and some of his friends will help build. And I have promised a party for after the float is completed."

I rolled my eyes. One more thing to contend with. Still . . . "It sounds like the matter has been taken out of my hands."

"Yes. If you will give the permission, I will take care of the rest."

"All right, go ahead. Just so long as you don't make me work on it."

Susana looked stern. "Where is your *entusiasmo?*"

"It left with the accountant."

"What?"

"Never mind. It was a bad joke."

"Oh. Well, do I indeed have the permIssion?"

"Yes. Fine. *Vaya con Dios.*"

"You are in a strange mood, no?"

"Very strange."

Susana sighed and consulted her pad. "The next matter is that of Jesse's grandmother."

"Why, is she going to ride on the float?"

"Elena, this is not funny! For days now you have promised to look at those paintings about the labor unions—"

"I know, Susana, but the woman is all the way up in Ojai, and I haven't had time." I glanced at Emily to see what effect this exchange was having on her. She was sitting up straighter, listening.

"Jesse tells me she is old and sick and needs the money."

I gripped the edge of the desk and closed my eyes, counting to ten.

Emily suddenly said, "What kind of paintings?"

"Paintings of the farm workers' struggle," Susana said. *"La Raza."* To me she added, "May I tell Jesse when you will go?"

"When I know when I will go, I will tell you. Then you may tell Jesse. But I do not know yet."

"Elena—"

"I do not know yet."

Susana's eyes flashed and she turned on her heel. "That is all, then."

I watched her leave, then bit down on my doughnut. It was filled with lemon cream. I hate lemon cream.

Emily was watching me, a spot of color on either cheek. "Elena, maybe I could help you about the paintings. I could drive to Ojai and look—"

"Thank you, Emily, but that's a job for a curator. I'll have to appraise them, and . . . *por Dios,* there's so much to do!"

"Maybe I could go with you. You said if I learned a skill . . ."

Feeling contrite at almost shutting her out, I said, "Of course. It's always nice to have someone else along on a drive like that. I'll let you know when I'm going."

She flushed even more and stood up. "Thank you, Elena. Thank you. And now I'd better go back to the gift shop; I left Mrs. Ramirez in charge, and you know she has trouble adding and subtracting."

I sat in the empty office, contemplating my unwanted doughnut. Now, what had caused Emily's sudden enthusiasm about going along with me to see the paintings? That woman, with her odd ways, interested me more and more. I would take her, as I'd promised; on a long drive it was possible I could draw her out about herself. And it *would* be good to have company.

I looked over at Ciro's manuscript. I had promised Dave Kirk I would keep my ears open around the trailer park, but that certainly didn't entail reading all those pages. If anyone should be doing it, it was the lieutenant himself.

The phone rang, and my intercom buzzed. I picked up the receiver and said, "Yes?"

"Elena?"

"Yes, Mama."

"Have you read it?"

"Ciro's manuscript? Partly."

"Well, what did you find out?"

"Mama, I'm not through yet."

"You haven't found out anything at all?"

"Not yet."

"Elena, you promised." Her tone was suddenly woebegone.

"I know, and I will finish it. But, Mama, I also have a job—"

"It isn't long. You could have read it last night."

"Last night I went to a party with Carlos."

"A fancy party?"

"Yes."

"Did you have a good time?"

"No."

"Then you would have been better off reading Ciro's book."

"Yes, I know."

"Elena, please."

Were those tears I heard in my mother's voice? I thought so. "All right. I'll read it today and call you as soon as I'm done."

"Thank you, Elena."

The intercom buzzed again. "Mama, I've got to go."

"Call me."

"Yes!" I pressed the button for the other line and said hello in none-too-polite tones.

"Elena, Dave Kirk."

"Yes, Dave."

"I'd like to have lunch with you. Something's come up, and we need to talk. Where can I meet you, and when?"

Did everyone think I merely spent my days in my office contemplating the arts? I considered briefly, then decided that I would take the afternoon off and read the manuscript at home. "How about in fifteen minutes at the Super-Rica?"

"That place at Milpas and Alphonse?"

"Yes."

"Make it half an hour and you've got a date."

I hung up, shaking my head. *I* had a date? *I* did? He was the one who'd asked—and the Santa Barbara County Sheriff's Department had better be paying for my lunch.

Five

THE SUPER-RICA was a former Orange Julius only a few blocks from my house, and it served the best burritos in town. I went past the order counter and looked out into the lattice-fenced courtyard that had once been a parking lot. It was early, and there were only a few people there. Dave Kirk sat at one of the tables, a bottle of Dos Equiis in front of him. When he saw me, he stood up as formally as is possible at a picnic table and motioned for me to be seated.

"Hi," he said. "I took the liberty of ordering for you."

Wonderful, I thought. I need an Anglo to order for me at my favorite tacqueria.

Kirk saw my frown but apparently thought it was due to the lack of something to drink. "Dos Equiis?"

"Please."

He went to the outside order window and returned shortly with a paper cup and a beer.

I poured the beer and sipped it, enjoying the warm sun on my shoulders. "You said something has come up."

"Yeah. Your mother may not be as far off base as I first assumed."

"My mother has never been off base in her life. But why are you admitting this now?"

"The autopsy results."

"And what were they?"

"Mr. Sisneros died of a cerebral hemorrhage."

"Meaning from injuries caused by a blow to the head. But didn't you more or less assume that yesterday?"

"Sure, but I always like to have official corroboration. The autopsy ruled out the possibility of a stroke or heart attack. The cause was simply the injuries he sustained when his head hit that planter box."

"I don't see where this is anything new, though. I mean anything you need to discuss with me."

"I'm coming to that. The autopsy also showed other things." Kirk finished his beer and gestured at mine. "You want another."

"Not yet. You go ahead."

"I'll check on our food while I'm up there." He went back to the order window, and I sat there tapping fingertips on the rough wood of the table, annoyed at the delay.

Kirk came back and slipped into his place on the bench opposite me. "Food in five minutes, they say."

The courtyard was starting to fill up now that the noontime rush was on. A man and woman in business attire came over and settled down at the other end of our long table. I glanced at them, wondering if it was wise to discuss Ciro's murder in such a public place, then decided—since they immediately started arguing in loud voices—that they wouldn't listen anyway.

"Where were we?" Kirk asked.

"The other things the autopsy showed."

"Well, one thing was possible evidence of foul play. Mr. Sisneros had bruises on his forearms, fresh ones. And he fell hard enough to on his back to rupture internal organs and damage his spine."

"What does that mean? That he was pushed?"

"Maybe, but there's a better possibility. The coroner says that from the shape and angle of the head wound, he could have been flipped on his back from the opposite side of the planter box, hitting his head on the way down."

"Flipped?"

"Yeah, like in a judo hold."

"Judo. . . . Ciro was a judo instructor at the Leisure Village rec center."

"Right."

"But then couldn't those bruises have happened in one of his classes? They can get pretty rough, you know."

"Possibly. One of the things I want to find out is when he last taught a class."

"Do you really think, since Ciro was an expert, that someone could have gotten him in a hold and taken him unawares?"

"I don't know. I guess it would depend on the circumstances."

I was silent for a moment, remembering a time a few years back when one of my boyfriends had been taking judo. He'd been trying to convince me I should try it, saying it would be good for me to have some knowledge of self-defense. I am notoriously unathletic, except when it comes to swimming, but to humor him, I'd allowed him to show me a few holds. He'd guided me through them and then let me try one. And I'd followed his instructions to a tee and flipped him right over my shoulder onto his back. He'd credited my success to beginner's luck coupled with the element of surprise, and I had had to agree with him.

Well, I thought now, what if someone had come up to Ciro and asked to be shown a judo hold? Could Ciro have been taken off guard, as my old boyfriend had? If it was someone he knew and had no reason to distrust, then probably yes. The person wouldn't even have had to have much knowledge of judo.

"It could have been an accident," I said. "Maybe he was demonstrating a hold for someone, and whoever it was flipped him by mistake. A person might panic and run away in a situation like that."

"That's true."

"But, according to my mother, someone had threatened him."

"Right again."

"So what do you want from me? I take it you're not telling me all this merely for my enlightenment."

"I want two things: I want you to find out when Ciro taught that last class, and which people in that trailer park studied judo. And I want you to ask around to see if anyone had quarreled with him recently."

"That's three things."

"Three things, two tasks. Will you?"

"Yes. But why can't you do this yourself?"

"It's as I told you yesterday—they don't want to cooperate with an Anglo cop. I went up there to get a list of the people who took the bus in to El Mercado, and the park manager, Adela Hernandez, practically threw me out of her office. She indicated she would prepare the list but that it might take ever-so-many days."

"Oh, that Adela. It's not you; she just doesn't like *any* Anglos."

"Well, whatever the reason, I suppose I could get tough with her. But why antagonize the residents when I have you to do it for me?"

"*I'm* going to antagonize them instead?"

"You know what I mean. And, in addition, you can ask questions without arousing suspicion the way I would. If the killer is someone in the park, he won't be alerted to the direction my investigation is taking."

Kirk's name came over the loudspeaker just then, and he hurried up to the order window to get our food. I sipped beer, steeling myself for some Anglo version of the Super-Rica's famous burrito but was pleasantly surprised when the lieutenant returned with their chorizo special, everything on it and then some.

"For an Anglo," I said, "you know what to order."

He grinned and handed me a stack of paper napkins. "I knew this place was near your house, so I figured you were a regular. I asked them what you usually had."

"Very clever of you."

"I'm a detective both on and off the job."

"But why so many paper napkins?"

His grin grew wider as he picked up his burrito. "The man behind the counter advised it. He says you are a very sloppy eater."

I decided to keep my promise to my mother and read the rest of Ciro's manuscript before driving up to the park to try to gather Kirk's information. Once home, I stretched out on the lounge chair under the big pepper tree in my backyard and skimmed through the remaining pages in a little over two hours. The manuscript ended abruptly just a few paragraphs into a chapter on the migrant labor camps, and I felt a disappointment akin to what I might experience if someone had cut the last few chapters out of a particularly good mystery novel. I wondered what Ciro had intended to do in the rest of the book, and then I realized he must have had an outline. No one could write something as complex as this without one.

I went into the house and called my mother to ask if Ciro had given her a copy of the outline. The phone rang and rang. Now where was she off to? It could have been any one of a number of places; my mother's appointed daily rounds ranged far and wide, from the rec center to the laundry room, from the supermarket to the public library.

I didn't want to wait to look at that outline—if Mama even had a copy.

At lunch Kirk had said I could take another look at Ciro's trailer and that I could pick up the key at the sheriff's department. I packed the manuscript in my tote bag, went by the sheriff's station—which was right off Route 101 on my way to Goleta—and then drove to Leisure Village.

The place seemed quieter than usual. Only a few people sat outside under their canopies or shade trees, and through the open doors of the rec center I saw that no one was at the pool or putting green. The people here were used to death—it wasn't uncommon for an elderly resident to suffer a heart attack, die in his or her sleep, or go away to the hospital and not return. But that kind of death was natural; what had happened to Ciro wasn't. The possibility of violence had touched the little community, and people were doubtless staying in the safety of their own homes.

All except my mother. There was no answer to my knock at her trailer door. I went back down the cul-de-sac to the rec center, where Adela Hernandez lived in an apartment behind the office off the entryway. Adela was at her desk, looking as sour and ill-used as ever. She was a tall, gaunt woman, probably in her sixties, with a prominent nose and black hair that was streaked with gray. Her eyes were dark and snapping, and they surveyed her small domain critically, ever on the alert for visitors who left their cars in the residents' parking slots or people who ventured into the pool without first passing through the footbath. When I came in, she looked up and gave me the grim twitch of her lips that passed for a smile. Adela didn't like many people, but for some reason she liked me. I didn't know whether to take that as a compliment or not.

"How are you today, Elena?" she asked. "Shouldn't you be at work?"

Even when she attempted to be pleasant, she sounded critical. I said, "I'm taking the afternoon off. Can I talk to you about something in private?"

"What, is it something about your mother? She's not sick, is she?"

"No, nothing like that."

"Don't tell me she can't afford to pay the rent on her space. I thought you girls took care of that—"

"It's not about my mother."

"Oh." Adela looked momentarily disappointed that there was no misfortune to fuel her poor opinion of the world. Then she stood up and said, "We can talk in my apartment."

I followed her to the door, then stopped, realizing I'd never been in there before. Surely I would have remembered it if I had.

The living room was crammed with shabby overstuffed furniture and cheap Mexican souvenirs. Piñatas hung from the ceiling; garish bullfighter paintings on velvet covered the walls. On shelves and tabletops stood ceramic burros, señorita dolls with flouncy skirts, toy guitars, decorative mariachis, and even a couple of *pelotas*—the baskets used in jai alai. The lampshades were actually shaped like sombreros, and serapes were draped like slipcovers over the furniture. The only nice things in the room, in fact, were a silver squash-blossom necklace, a tea set, and a few knives, spoons, and forks that sat on the coffee table next to a rag and a can of silver polish. Probably she hid them away when she wasn't cleaning them.

All in all, it boggled the mind. I stood in the doorway, gaping. When Adela turned and caught my expression, she gave me another of those grim mouth-twitches.

"It startles you, doesn't it?" she said.

"Uh, yes."

"My husband and I owned a shop on Olvera Street in Los Angeles for over thirty years. Souvenirs. Postcards. It was a good living. When he died and I moved up here, I couldn't part with all the things. Having them here, it feels like he's still with me in some way." She motioned for me to sit on a serape-covered chair, and I did, still marveling at her incredibly bad taste.

"So," Adela said, "what is this private talk about?"

"Ciro Sisneros. Do you know when he taught his last judo class?"

The question surprised her, because she blinked. "Why do you need to know that?"

"Well, you must have heard that my mother has this idea that he was murdered."

Adela glowered. "The entire park has heard it—in detail. Your mother has too much imagination for her own good. I'm not going to aid either of you in this."

"In what?"

"I know what you're doing, Elena Oliverez. I read the papers, and I also heard plenty of talk about you solving that Frank De Palma's murder."

"Then surely you want to help."

"I do not. Stirring things up, talking of murder—it's not good for this park. People come here in their retirement. They want things quiet, well ordered. It's my job to see that they are. I won't help you stir up a hornet's nest."

"I'm not trying to do that." Then, in a moment of sudden inspiration, I added, "What I'm trying to do is prove to my mother that Ciro *wasn't* murdered, so she'll stop all this talk and go back to her crocheting, or whatever she's taken up lately."

"Tapestry."

"What?"

"Tapestry. There's a workshop over at the Goleta Community Center. She's there most afternoons from two to four."

That explained her absence. I really ought to keep closer track of Mama's activities, I decided.

"A lot of foolishness," Adela said. "A new interest every month or two. She'll finish that tapestry and then be on to something new."

Personally, I didn't find that bad at all; Mama's varied interests kept her active. But then, different people fed on different things. Nick, for instance, had a long-term and all-consuming interest in jogging. Adela, I had to assume, thrived on carping and complaining.

"Well, anyway," I said, "won't you help me convince her that Ciro wasn't murdered?"

"How is his judo schedule going to do that?"

"I'm not certain," I said vaguely. "It's just a hunch I have."

"Hunches!" But she got up and went out to the office, returning with a large looseleaf notebook. She spread it on the coffee table, paged through it, and said, "Ciro's last judo class was a week ago today. He would have taught from ten to twelve this morning if . . ." She crossed herself.

A week ago. Then the class couldn't account for those fresh bruises. "Did Ciro ever teach anyone privately?"

Adela shut the notebook. "Certainly not. It is not permitted, using the park facilities for one's own profit."

"I didn't necessarily mean for money."

"Well, the answer is still no."

"Can I have the list of the people who took Ciro's classes?"

"I'm sorry, but that's the property of the trailer park."

"Adela, it can't be of any use to you anymore."

"Be that as it may, I can't give it out."

She was beginning to get on my nerves, so quickly I asked my other question. "Do you know if any of the residents had quarreled with Ciro recently?"

"Why do you ask that?"

"The same reason—a hunch."

"Hmm. Well, I'm sorry, but I can't talk about the residents. It wouldn't be right for the park manager—"

"Please, Adela."

"I'm sorry, but no. Even if anyone had been annoyed with Ciro, it wouldn't have come to murder, if that's what you're thinking."

"I didn't say—"

"You didn't have to. I know what you're after, Elena Oliverez. You don't fool me one bit. You think you'll play detective and find yourself another killer."

I was silent.

"No one killed Ciro, Elena. He was a very sweet man. No one would want to hurt him."

The kind words surprised me, as did Adela's expression—a downturning of her lips that I supposed was as close to grief as the sour old woman ever got. All the same, I wanted to get out of this tacky apartment and away from her critical pronouncements. I thanked her for the information, got up, and went outside. Mama was coming across the lawn in front of the rec center with Nick, pulling his little grocery cart, in tow. I waved and went to join them.

Six

"THERE YOU ARE," I said to Mama. "How was your tapestry class?"

She looked surprised. "Who told you about that?"

"Adela."

"I should have known. That woman pokes her nose into everything."

"It isn't a secret, is it?"

She shrugged and turned to Nick. "Let me have those avocados. I'll fix us some nice guacamole for before dinner. And the tomatoes, please."

Nick rummaged through the bags in the little cart. "The onions are yours too."

"Don't forget the chicken. It's for dinner; you're invited, if you care to come."

"I accept. But you owe me five dollars. What you gave me didn't cover your part of the bill."

"What, are you trying to get rich off of me? I figured it to the penny."

"If I had every penny you *didn't* figure into it, I could run off to Las Vegas."

"And be lonely there."

I smiled at them. Every few days they did their grocery shopping together. And every few days they bickered over who had paid his share. As for the invitation to dinner, Nick ate most of his meals—to say nothing of spending most of his nights—at my mother's. His trailer, Mama claimed, was too small and crowded with weights and health food.

It made me glad, seeing how happy my mother was. And I loved Nick for bringing this joy into her life. My father had died when I was only three—an explosion in the cannery where he was working—and Mama had spent the next twenty years working as a domestic, cleaning other people's houses during the day and ours at night. But somehow she had always had time for my sister Cariota and me—time for helping with homework and sewing badges onto Brownie Scout uniforms and planning how to save enough money for a dress to the prom. Now that Cariota and I were through school and self-supporting, it was nice to be able to take care of Mama for a change. Not that she asked more than the rent on her trailer space; Mama was fiercely independent, and she'd passed on that quality to both of her daughters.

She collected her bundles from Nick, warned him not to be later than five, and set off toward the trailer with me tagging along behind.

"So what's this with the tapestry class, Mama?" I asked. "Why are you acting like it's some big secret?"

She struggled to get her key out of her purse, and I took the bundles from her. "Because I am making a wonderful tapestry. Christ ascending the cross."

Oh no, I thought. It's for me.

She got the door open and we went into the trailer. It was hot and musty-smelling, and Mama went around opening the louvered windows.

"Christ ascending the cross," I said.

"Yes. It is beautiful. And very large."

Madre de Dios, I could picture a religious tapestry covering the entire wall of my living room. "How large?"

"Large." Mama gestured widely. "At least six feet by eight feet."

I almost breathed a sigh of relief. It would by no stretch

of the imagination fit in my tiny house. Then I remembered Carlota's big apartment in Minneapolis. How awful! I'd have to warn her. . . .

"You don't like homemade things, Elena?" Mama asked.

"I didn't say that."

"Maybe you don't like religious things."

"Well, Christ ascending the cross isn't exactly a pleasant scene."

"It is not meant to be pleasant. It is to remind us, teach us a lesson. And you a good Catholic."

"Mama—"

"I know. Not such a good Catholic."

"Mama!"

She was grinning wickedly at me, and I realized my leg was being pulled—had been pulled for a few minutes now.

"Who's the tapestry really for?"

"What?" She raised her eyebrows in feigned innocence and went into the kitchen.

"Who?"

"The church."

I felt a rush of relief. "Mama, that's nice."

"I think so. It is not a wealthy church, and something is needed for behind the altar."

"So why the secrecy?"

She began to peel the avocados. "Because the church doesn't know they're getting it yet."

I nodded and went to help her with the guacamole. The church didn't know yet. What a surprise it would be. I wondered if I should talk to Father Quitoriano, prepare him for this gift. But then I decided I'd rather watch the fun. Besides, Mama's ability at crafts was better than the average.

As I chopped tomatoes, I said, "I finished what there was of Ciro's manuscript."

Instantly she became alert. "What did you find?"

"Not much. I need the outline for the rest of it. Did he leave a copy with you?"

"I gave you all I had."

"Well, that's all right. Dave Kirk let me have the key to Ciro's trailer; I'll go over there after dinner and make a thorough search."

"You've talked to that policeman, then?"

"Yes. It seems you may be right; he's not admitting it, but I know he thinks it could have been murder."

Mama looked at me, triumphant but also a little sad. "See?"

"Yes, I see." We were silent for a moment, preparing vegetables. Then I said, "Mama, Dave Kirk wants me to find out a few things."

"Like what?"

"If anyone around here had quarreled with Ciro before he died. I asked Adela Hernandez, but she said she couldn't talk about the residents."

Mama snorted. "Adela, trying to be important again."

"Well, do you know of anyone? You were pretty close to Ciro."

She thought, staring out the little window above the sink, her knife dangling limp from her hand. "Well, there was Mary Jaramillo. Mary and Ciro never got along."

Mary was the vigorous, heavyset woman in her early seventies I'd seen outside the rec center the day before. She owned two purebred Persian cats, which she dragged around to regional cat shows. "Why not?"

"Mary is an amateur historian. She felt there were inaccuracies in Ciro's work and was always taking him to task for them."

"It doesn't sound like something she'd kill him over."

"Yes, but on the other hand, the person who threatened Ciro said it was because of his book."

"True. Anyone else?"

"Sam Walters and Ciro weren't speaking."

Sam Walters was the big Anglo who was married to a Chicana. "Why not?"

"Ciro was philosophizing one night out by the pool. That means he'd had a few gin-and-tonics and wasn't watching what he was saying. He made some negative remarks about mixed marriages in front of Sam and Gloria." Mama gave me a penetrating look, and I knew she was trying to gauge if I was seeing any Anglos lately.

I ignored the look. "I thought Ciro was a tactful man."

"He was. What he said was not about all mixed marriages; he was commenting on a specific few he knew of that hadn't worked out. But Sam Walters flew into a temper and almost got into a fight with him. Since then, they hadn't spoken."

"How long ago was this?"

"About six weeks."

I thought about Sam and Gloria, and their shocked expressions when I'd seen them in the crowd the day before. Still, such expressions could be put on for others' benefit. And Sam—a big, rugged man, in spite of some fifty pounds' excess weight—had an explosive temper when crossed.

"Then, of course," Mama said, "there's Joe Garcia."

"Ciro's neighbor."

"Yes, the little *redrojo*. He doesn't fit in here."

"Besides the fact that he's a twerp, why not?"

"Well, for one thing, he's too young. Only fifty. And for another, he seems to have gotten this place mixed up with a swinging-singles complex."

"What does he do to make you think that?"

"Plays his stereo very loud. Rock-and-roll music. Drools over the women at the pool. Me, even. Can you imagine anyone having the nerve to drool over *me*?"

"Only Nick."

"Do I hear my name being taken in vain?" Nick came into the trailer, clad in a clean pair of running shorts and T-shirt, obviously in response to the formal invitation to dinner.

"Elena says you drool," Mama said.

"Mama—"

"Sometimes," Nick admitted. He patted me on the head and then reached over to sample the half-mixed guacamole.

Mama pulled the bowl away and glared at him.

I said, "Are you sure you should eat that, you old food faddist?"

"I follow no fads; I just make the rules. Tonight the rule is guacamole." He plucked a taco chip from a dish Mama had set out and popped it into his mouth, crunching loudly. "So what is happening about Ciro's murder?"

Mama certainly had at least one person convinced. I told him what Dave Kirk had told me, and then about what Mama and I had been discussing.

"Joe Garcia," Nick said thoughtfully. "Ciro was really mad at him—and vice versa"

"Why?"

"The rock-and-roll music. He played his stereo all the time. Ciro couldn't work, and he complained, first to Joe and then to Adela Hernandez. Joe got plenty worked up over it, and all he did was turn the thing up louder. You could hear it all the way down here, and that's four trailers away."

"But would Joe *kill* someone because he'd complained to Adela?"

"Who knows, with these hot-tempered young fellows?"

Young. Fifty years old, and Nick thought Joe Garcia a young fellow. At this rate, he'd consider me a babe in diapers until at least thirty-five. The thought was very appealing.

"Does Joe Garcia know judo?" I asked.

"I don't know," Nick said. "Why?"

"Because Dave Kirk thinks Ciro was flipped in a judo hold before he hit his head on the planter and died."

"Oh." Nick looked a little edgy.

"Yes. There was something about the way he was lying and the type of injuries he'd sustained, plus the fact he taught the judo classes here in the park. Who do you know who's studied judo?" Nick was the ideal person to ask, since he had his fingertips on the athletic pulse of the park.

"A lot of people." He glanced uneasily at Mama

Unperturbed, she said, "Even Nick."

"Gabriela . . ." But he looked relieved to have it out in the open.

I smiled at him, this gentle man who had finally brought my mother happiness. "Well, I certainly don't suspect *you*."

"Oh." His expression became somewhat crestfallen. I supposed for a quiet-living type like Nick, being suspected of a murder—especially by your girlfriend's daughter—would be almost flattering.

Mama took the guacamole into the living room, and I followed with the chips. "Nick," she said, "please pour the wine."

We all sat down and attacked the guacamole furiously, as if we hadn't eaten for days. After a few minutes, Mama said, "Elena, I still think there's something in that manuscript that would give us an idea who did this thing to Ciro."

I nodded in agreement, my mouth full. "Either there or in his trailer. After dinner I'll go over there and look."

Ciro's trailer was stuffy with the heat that had built up during the day. A fly buzzed angrily at one of the windows over the desk, so I cranked it open to release the insect. Then I switched on the desk lamp and looked around.

The box of manuscript pages was still next to the typewriter. I took them out and looked through them, but found only the originals of those I'd already read. Where, I wondered, would Ciro have kept the outline? Probably in the four-drawer file cabinet that stood against the opposite wall.

I went over there and opened the top drawer. It was full of file folders, all with neatly typed labels—correspondence, expenses, taxes, legal affairs, even one for manuals and warranties on his appliances. The only file that might contain something of interest to me was the one that held correspondence, but when I went through it, I found only letters that appeared to be from friends or people who had read his books. In none was there mention of a threatening phone call.

The next drawer held files on books that had already been published—contracts, correspondence with editors, royalty statements, and copies of reviews. I shut it and opened the third drawer.

This was devoted exclusively to the book Ciro had been working on at the time of his death. The first folder contained the outline I was looking for, and after that there were individual files for each chapter. I scanned the outline, then sat down cross-legged on the floor and began going through the research material in each file, starting with the chapter where the manuscript had ended. And within a short time I realized something was wrong here.

There were gaps in the chronology, whole segments of time for which there were no notes or photocopies of printed research materials. One folder—on chapter eight, "The Great Labor Crisis"—was completely empty. It looked as if the files had been carefully searched and certain selected material removed.

But how had someone gotten in here to do that? And when? Probably not before Ciro had died, and since then the trailer had been sealed and the key kept in the possession of the sheriff's department. Of course, someone might have had an extra key; I'd have to ask my mother if she knew anyone Ciro would entrust one to. But if the person hadn't had a key . . .

I began to search the trailer for a means of entry. And quickly found it, in the bedroom, where the window had been forced, breaking two of the louvers. Whoever did it had replaced the screen, probably hoping the broken glass would go unnoticed, but the screen wasn't properly attached, and when I touched it, it clattered to the ground outside.

I went back to the living room and stood looking at the files spread out on the floor. The only way to figure out what the intruder had been after was to go through these files, listing the gaps in the chronology, then find someone who could tell me what historical events belonged in those periods. Then maybe I'd have some sort of clue.

I sat down on the floor again, noting that it was already after eleven, and began making a list on one of Ciro's legal pads. At midnight my mother knocked on the door and asked if I was all right. I said I was fine. Then she wanted to bring me a snack. I turned it down, telling her I'd work a while longer, then go home and call her in the morning. She withdrew, sounding a little annoyed.

The work was more time-consuming than I'd originally thought, and before I realized, it was after 2:00 A.M. My eyes burned, and my limbs ached from sitting on the floor. I got up, stretched, and looked longingly at the couch. Maybe a short nap would help. I'd always been able to set my mental clock so I'd awaken at whatever time I wanted to; I'd lie down and set it for three.

Sleep came quickly, and with it came dreams. They were the kind where you are very aware you're dreaming yet powerless to wake yourself and halt the unpleasant events that are taking place. First I was standing in the entry of the Rodriguezes' big house at the winery, in front of the stone chair supported by griffins. The griffins began to stir their stone wings and snap their sharply sculpted fangs. I backed away as they rose up, shrugging off the chair, becoming larger every moment—larger than me, until they filled the entry. . . .

I turned and ran. And suddenly I was at the museum, in the courtyard, at the edge of the fountain. Only it wasn't just a little fountain anymore but a great lake with rough waters that lapped at the sides and spilled over onto the ground, wetting my feet. Carlos and Susana were on the other side of the water, and they were laughing at me, pointing at my feet. Carlos had his arm around Susana, and as they laughed, their faces turned into devils' masks. A stench came off the water in the fountain, a musty smell. Skunk?

Skunk. That was it. There were skunks swimming in the fountain. No, not skunks. Something worse. Gas . . .

Gas!

I sat up straight, awake now, coughing and choking. The smell was all around me, and for a moment I didn't know where I was. Then I remembered I was on the couch in Ciro's trailer. And that the trailer had a gas hookup that could leak.

I jumped off the couch and ran across the room to where I thought the door was. But I was still disoriented by sleep, and I banged into Ciro's desk, hurting my hip. I whirled, coughing and fighting down nausea, and ran toward the other wall, feeling my way along it until I found the door handle. It stuck, and it was several seconds before I remembered to turn the lock. I heaved the door open, stumbled down the steps, and collapsed on the little lawn, sucking in great breaths of fresh air.

In a moment I raised my head and looked back at the trailer. Ciro's outline and notes were in there, as well as the list I'd spent all evening compiling. Perhaps when the place aired out, I could go back and retrieve them. . . .

There was an odd sound, a whooshing and then a thump. I'd never heard such a noise before, but instinctively I knew what it was. I got to my feet and started running. Across the cul-de-sac, into the shelter of the opposite trailer.

The thump was followed by a bang, and then flames shot skyward. The night was lit up as if someone had turned on a neon sign. Red neon. Red and gold and orange, engulfing Ciro's trailer—where minutes ago I'd been lying asleep.

Seven

"REALLY, MAMA, I'M all right."

"You don't look all right." Her face hovered over mine.

"But I am!" I started to sit up on her couch, where she and Nick had more or less laid me out.

My mother pushed me back, as if this were some sort of wrestling match.

"Mama, damn it, let me up!"

"Gabriela," Nick said from behind her, "let Elena up. She looks all right to me."

"Mrs. Oliverez, she really appears to be unharmed." The last voice was Dave Kirk's. He must have just gotten there.

Mama said, "Don't tell me how to deal with my child, Lieutenant Kirk." But she gave me one last penetrating look and then released me.

I sat up and ran my fingers through my curls, then looked around. The little living room was jammed with people—several of the neighbors, as well as my mother, Nick, and Dave Kirk.

Of course, all this uproar was over nothing. When Mama and Nick had found me in the crowd across the street from the burning trailer, I'd been fine. But they'd panicked and hauled me back here. And then Mama had proceeded to carry on as if I were on my deathbed. Now everyone was watching me, and I felt embarrassed.

Dave Kirk seemed to sense my discomfiture. He began

herding people toward the door, telling them I would be all right. When the last had gone, he came over to me and sat down on the other end of the couch. "What happened?" he asked.

"A gas leak. Luckily, I smelled it and got out before the explosion. Probably the trapped gas was touched off by something like the pilot light on the stove."

"Maybe." Suddenly he looked preoccupied.

"Aren't you going to ask me what I found in there?"

"Huh? Oh, I wasn't aware you were looking for anything."

"What, do you think I go around sleeping on other people's couches for pleasure? I *do* have a home, you know, and I'd like to be there right now—"

"Hey, take it easy." He put a hand on my arm and smiled at me. His brown eyes, usually so bland and unreadable, were filled with concern. I smiled back, deciding my initial guess about Kirk had been right; he was definitely interested in me.

"You didn't tell me you were asleep in there," Mama said.

"When did I have the chance to get a word in edgewise? Right now all I want is to go home. I'm exhausted, and I want to take a hot bath and then go to bed."

"You'll stay here," she said.

"No, I won't. I'm going home to my own bed."

"What if you have a relapse?"

"Por Dios, of *what?* I'm not sick. I'm not even hurt."

"You know, Mrs. Oliverez," Kirk said smoothly, "Elena's right. She's better off at home. But since you're worried, I tell you what—I'll drive her there to make sure she arrives okay."

"My car—" I began.

"I'll bring you back for it tomorrow."

Mama smiled. "Thank you, Lieutenant. I'm glad someone looks out for my little girl."

I was already across the room and halfway out the door.

Kirk followed me. Mama came close behind him, calling out all sorts of instructions and admonishments.

"I can drive myself," I said through gritted teeth.

"Humor your mother. If she looks out later and sees your car is gone, she'll probably turn up at your house and then you'll never get any sleep. Besides, you can tell me what you found out on the way."

I sighed, but followed him to the unmarked car that sat next to my VW in the visitors' parking area. The fire trucks had already departed, and although there were still a few people lingering in front of the rec center, most of the lights in the surrounding trailers were starting to go out. I got into the car and listened to the crackling of the radio as Kirk got in on his side.

"Is that"—I motioned at the radio—"how you knew about the explosion?"

"Yeah." He turned the car toward the freeway. "It's odd, isn't it?"

"You mean that Ciro's trailer should explode and burn the day after he died? It's a lot odder than you know." And I proceeded to tell him about the gaps in the research material and the list I'd been making.

"Can you remember anything of what you wrote down?" he asked.

"Maybe I can reconstruct it, but I don't know. I was pretty tired and working more or less mechanically. I'll try, and let you know." I paused, then added, "I guess this means that gas leak was no accident."

"Probably not."

"And it probably wasn't ignited by anything as innocent as a pilot light."

"Maybe. We'll see what the arson squad says. Who knew you were in there?"

"Only Mama and Nick. But anybody could have seen that the light was on."

He nodded. "Find out anything else while you were at the trailer park?"

"Only that those bruises on Ciro's arms couldn't have been from a judo class." I explained about my talk with Adela Hernandez, and then about the three people Mama had mentioned who'd quarreled with Ciro.

"Can you check out those people for me tomorrow?" he asked.

"How?"

"Go around and talk with them."

"What am I supposed to say? 'I'm here to find out if you murdered Ciro and then tried to blow me up'?"

Kirk laughed wryly and braked as the freeway ended in Santa Barbara. "I think you can handle it more subtly than that. But it ought to be easy for you to strike up a conversation with anyone at the park. Tonight's events have made you a kind of celebrity."

"It's not the sort of celebrity I've always dreamed of."

"No, I guess not."

"And I *do* have a job, you know. Contrary to appearances, that museum doesn't just run itself."

"Try anyway." He turned left, heading toward my neighborhood. The small houses there were dark, the solid working-class people all abed—as any sane person would be at this hour.

When we rounded the corner of my street, I said, "Okay, I'll try. But I can't promise how soon it will be."

"I'm not worried." He brought the car to a stop in front of my house.

"Oh? And why is that?"

"You're just naturally nosy."

I got out and slammed the car door. When I was halfway up my walk, Kirk called after me, "Let me know when you want to fetch your auto."

I turned, glaring. "You know, I think I'd rather take a cab up there. I'd rather *walk*."

His laughter was very loud in the predawn silence. Across the street, Mrs. Nunez's front curtain twitched. I knew she was a poor sleeper who often wandered around the house late at night, peering out the windows for burglars. If she'd recognized Kirk's car as the unmarked sheriff's vehicle it so obviously was, her round-the-clock reconnaissance would really have paid off this time.

My alarm went off as usual at eight that morning—an hour that seemed a lot earlier than it normally did. *"Maldito,"* I muttered, rolling over and lunging at the clock. It slipped from my grasp and fell to the carpet, still trilling. For a moment I cursed its sturdiness—it was an old Big Ben I'd had since childhood, an indestructible monster whose loud ticking somehow comforted me. But then the alarm stopped and the clock lay there looking abused. I snuggled down under the covers, promising myself ten more minutes, and soon was back asleep.

When I woke again, it was after ten. I jumped out of bed in a panic, reaching for my robe. The museum, I thought. I wasn't there to open up, and all the people would be waiting . . . .

And then I remembered that two weeks ago I'd decided Susana's probationary period should end and had given her a key to the alarm system. It had been a source of pride to her, indicating not only that she'd learned her job well but that I also didn't feel any of her former husband's thieving habits had rubbed off on her. And for me, it had been a relief, an abdication of a sometimes overwhelming responsibility.

I tied the robe around me and sat down on the bed, first replacing my alarm clock on the table and then dialing the museum on the extension phone. The call went unanswered for several rings, and when Susana finally picked it up, there was a lot of noise and laughter in the background.

"What's going on there?" I asked.

"The building of the float. Did you sleep late this morning? It was on the news about the bombing of that trailer, so I did not feel I should disturb you."

"Yes, I slept in. You've already started building the float?"

"Of course. It is Wednesday; the parade is Saturday night. You were not hurt in the explosion, I trust?"

"No. What's the float going to look like?"

"It will be a giant one of Jesse's *camaleones*. What were you doing in that trailer?"

"Looking for something. Who decided what the float should be?"

"I did, with Jesse's advice. What were you looking for?"

"I'll explain that later. How much is this float costing us?"

"Not one cent more than Mr. Bowman's contribution. When will you come in to work?"

"I don't know yet. Are you sure it won't cost more?"

"No, even the beer is coming out of the money we have been given. Do you intend to see Jesse's grandmother today?"

"I don't know. Beer, at this hour?"

"No, later." There was a sudden shriek in the background. "Susana, what's happened?"

Silence. It sounded like she'd clamped her hand over the mouthpiece.

"Susana!"

When she came back on the line, her voice was breathy and rushed. "It is nothing, Elena. Do not trouble yourself. But I must go now." And she hung up.

I sat there holding the receiver and considering. I could call back. I could run over there. But it probably *was* nothing, and if I went to work, I'd end up stuck with a thousand minor tasks and phone calls left over from the previous afternoon. Besides, hadn't Susana indicated she was ready for more responsibility? Let her try her wings today; if she failed, it would be on her head, not mine.

No, I thought, what I'd do was have a couple of leisurely

cups of coffee and then call Dave Kirk and get him to drive me to the trailer park to retrieve my car. In return for the favor, I'd talk to the three people he wanted me to.

After all, I couldn't hold a grudge against the lieutenant. He was absolutely right about me: I *am* incurably nosy.

Eight

I WAVED GOOD-BYE to Kirk and watched him turn in front of the rec center and drive off. He had been pleasant but unusually silent all the way to Leisure Village, and while he seemed pleased I was going to talk to the three suspects—or whatever they would be called in police jargon—he also seemed uninterested and remote. Probably his mind was on one of his other cases, or maybe even on a personal matter.

As I crossed the park toward my mother's cul-de-sac, where Joe Garcia's trailer sat next to the burned-out wreck of Ciro's, I wondered about Dave Kirk. He was unmarried—that I knew because my mother had asked him once. But I didn't know if he had ever been married before, or if he was involved or living with anyone. Mama had found out that he was a graduate of the California Polytechnic State University at San Luis Obispo; that he'd been with the Santa Barbara Police Department for eight years, which would make him around thirty; that he had an apartment within walking distance of the beach; that he was a Gemini. Trust my mother to glean as many details as possible about a man she thought might be interested in me—even if the man was an Anglo.

The ruin of Ciro's trailer looked ugly in the morning light. What remained were twisted metal beams rising from the cinderblock foundation. The smell of fire and chemicals lingered in the air, and even the trunk of a nearby shade tree was scorched. Joe Garcia's trailer was to the right of Ciro's space, and the wiry little man was standing on the grass that separated the two, staring at the side of his.

When I went up to him, I saw why he was contemplating the trailer. The side closest to Ciro's was browned and blistered from the heat of the flames. Garcia heard my footsteps and turned, his swarthy face creased in a peevish frown. His skin looked the fifty years he supposedly was, but his hair was jet black, as if he used Grecian Formula on it, and blow-dried back in an unsuccessful attempt to hide a bald spot.

"The fire did a lot of damage, didn't it?" I said, motioning at his trailer.

"Yeah. I'm only renting this dump, so I guess it's up to the park owners to fix it."

"Oh, I'm sure they will."

He shrugged. "With my luck, who knows?" Then his eyes moved over me appraisingly and he went a little slackjawed. He probably thought he was giving me a sexy look, but all it did was make me realize what Mama had meant about his drooling.

He said, "You're Gabriela Oliverez's girl, aren't you? The one who was in the trailer when it exploded."

"Hardly. I mean, yes, I'm Elena Oliverez. But I wasn't inside, not then. If I had been, I wouldn't be standing here right now." Saying this made me shiver slightly.

"Oh, right. I meant you *had* been inside."

"Yes, I was."

The pseudo-sexy look was gone now, replaced by wariness. "Why?"

"Why was I in there?"

"Yeah."

"I was going over some things for my mother. She was Ciro's best friend, you know."

He shrugged again, as if to indicate doubt that Ciro had had a friend. "What sort of things?"

"Papers."

"That book?"

"What book?"

He looked surprised at my response but didn't pursue it. "Does the fire department know what caused it? There were a couple of official-looking guys out here a while ago, poking around."

"I guess not yet."

"What did it seem like to you?"

"A gas leak."

Garcia stared at the wreckage, looking thoughtful. "That makes sense."

"I guess you'll miss Ciro," I said after a moment.

"What?"

"Well, he was your neighbor."

"Yeah, and a damned nuisance, too."

"How?"

"He was always complaining about something or other."

"Oh, I remember he did say something to Mama about your loud rock music."

"Rock music!" Garcia snorted. "Makes it sound like the kind of crap they're recording today. I like the classics."

"Like what?"

"The Beatles, the Stones. The Beach Boys."

Classics. "Well, maybe if you had the stereo turned up loud—"

"Loud! What's loud? I got to be able to hear it, don't I?" His voice had risen, and I realized he'd been talking louder than normal all along. Joe Garcia was probably a little deaf—and too vain to wear a hearing aid or admit the fact to anyone. "Other than your differences about the music, how did you get along with Ciro?"

He calmed down, and the wary look returned. "Why?"

"I'm just curious. He seemed like such a nice man."

"He was all right." Garcia began moving toward the door of his trailer.

"Why do you think somebody killed him?"

His steps slowed, and he turned back to me. "Killed him? I thought he fell."

"There's a rumor going around that somebody caused that fall."

"Jesus, I didn't know that."

"Well, it's true."

"Jesus." His hands clenched and unclenched spasmodically. "What do the cops think?"

"They're suspicious."

"They're not saying that I . . .?"

"The two of you *did* have your differences."

"But nothing like that! Come on, do I look like the kind of guy who would kill somebody?" He spread his arms wide, trying to force his face into innocent lines. What it did was make him look guilty as could be.

"Do you know anything about judo, Mr. Garcia?"

"Judo? What the hell does that have to do with anything?"

"Do you?"

"No. Why should I?"

"Were you home last night when the trailer blew up?"

"Sure I was home. I mean, no, I wasn't home. I was over at the Low-Ball Bar. There's a chick who works there that I see."

"You must have come home sometime. The bars close at two."

"What is this? What're you getting at?"

"I just wondered if you'd seen or heard anyone around Ciro's trailer before the explosion."

He looked at me for a moment, then went to the door of the trailer. "I didn't see anyone. I was with my lady friend all night—at her place."

"Who is your friend?"

He flushed and stepped inside. "I don't have to answer that." And he closed the door.

I waited to see if he would come back out, then started slowly down the cul-de-sac. Joe Garcia was awfully nervous about the subject of Ciro, and I'd be sure to pass on the information about the lady friend at the Low-Ball to Kirk so he could check out the story. But *did* Garcia look like the kind of man who would kill somebody? I didn't know; killers came in all sizes and shapes, as well as both sexes.

I decided to make Mary Jaramillo's trailer my next stop. When I looked through the screen door as I knocked, I saw she was home, feeding a catnip leaf to one of her Persians. The cat tumbled on the floor, a great cloud of gray fur that rolled over and over, begging like a dog. The other cat, a white one, lay on the couch looking impervious to all this nonsense. It had those flat purebred Persian features and a dignified air that made me think of a British colonel from the days when the Empire ruled the world. I half-expected it to say, "Tut-tut."

Mary gave the other cat another leaf and called for me to come in. "Elena, are you all right? I was worried when I heard about you being in that explosion. What were you doing in Ciro's trailer anyway?"

Mary was a large woman with a huge shelf of bosom. As usual, she was wearing one of her flowing muumuus, trying to project a maternal air to go with her overblown figure. But I knew that the only ones who got much mothering from her were the cats.

"I'm okay," I said, sitting down next to the British colonel and stroking him. He turned his head and gave me a haughty yellow stare, then looked back at his sibling, who, to the colonel's way of thinking, was obviously making an ass of himself over a mere leaf.

Mary extended a box of chocolates to me and, when I declined, heaved herself into a lounger, setting the box on her lap. I looked around the room. Like the one in Ciro's trailer, it was lined with bookshelves. Most of the volumes were on history, and there was an entire shelf of back issues of a state historical journal I'd subscribed to for a while when I was in college. Interestingly, none of the books were ones that Ciro had written.

When she had arranged the voluminous folds of her garment, Mary said, "But what *were* you doing at Ciro's, Elena? And so late at night?"

I'd already decided on a plausible story to tell Mary, one that would easily get her talking about her differences with Ciro. "Going through his files on his book about the Depression."

Mary frowned. "But why, *niña?* You don't know anything about history."

"Well, I do, a little. I had a few courses from Ciro when I was at the university. But actually all I was doing was organizing. Someone's going to have to finish the book, and Mama wants to make sure all the files are in order before that person takes over."

Mary sat up straighter, looking alert. "Who's going to do it? I suppose Gabriela has already decided that."

"I don't think she's got anything to say about it. That's up to the publisher."

"Nonsense, *niña.* Your mother is Ciro's heir, and the executor of his will. She gets everything."

That surprised me. "How do you know?"

"I witnessed the will, several months ago."

"I don't think Mama knows that."

"Of course she does. Ciro left a copy with her for safekeeping."

I'd have to ask Mama about that—soon. "Well, be that as it may, the book will have to be finished. What about you? You're an authority on local history. Would you be interested?"

"I would not." She sniffed indignantly, her hand hovering over the chocolate box.

"Why not?"

She chose a foil-covered candy and tossed the crumpled wrapper to the floor. The gray cat went after it, batting with its paws. Beside me, the colonel looked away and practically sighed, as if to say, "Oh, really now!"

"Why not?" I asked again.

Around a mouthful of chocolate, Mary said, "I could not do it, because I would have to rewrite the entire book. Ciro was exceptionally careless about his facts. And his viewpoint was faulty."

"How so? I thought he'd received a lot of positive critical attention."

"Of course he had—from the East Coast establishment. Anglo critics. Jewish critics. What do they know? The fact remains that his treatment of Chicanos was abominable. He portrayed us in a very unfavorable light. And don't think I didn't take him to task for it."

I thought back to the books of Ciro's that I'd read, trying to recall this abominable treatment, but nothing came to mind.

Mary stuffed another chocolate into her mouth and chewed vigorously. "You know, I have a theory that Ciro was not too proud of being Chicano. He always acted as if he was above the rest of us, with his fancy education and his career at the university and his damned books."

"I never noticed that."

"Well, Elena, I don't like to bring it up, but with your schooling and your Anglo boyfriends, you're no better than Ciro." She spoke through set teeth, as if she would like to bite me. Angry lights flashed in her eyes, and for the first time I saw that this big, comfortable-looking woman concealed a lot of rage under that motherly exterior.

Slowly I said, "I don't think an education automatically puts us out of touch with our heritage."

"Oh, don't you?" She smiled unpleasantly, like the ghastly grin of a jack-o'-lantern.

"No."

"It gives you ideas, makes you think you're better than your people."

"How can you say that? Aren't you educated yourself? Look at all the books you have." I waved my hand at the shelves.

"I'm self-educated. I never had the time for fancy colleges. Or the money."

Why did I feel the need to justify myself to this angry, bitter woman? "I wouldn't call UCSB a 'fancy college.' And I worked for my money every day I was enrolled there. As for now, what, do you think I'm doing if not working for our people?"

She brushed my question aside with a flick of her chocolate-stained hand. "Don't tell me if the Metropolitan Museum of Art so much as whistled that you wouldn't be packed and gone within an hour. You're probably where you are because it was the only job you were offered."

She was right on the latter point—at the time I graduated, curator's jobs were hard to come by. But she was dead wrong about the former. I was proud of my museum and the long way we'd come in the five years since our founding. We would go even farther under my guidance. The job was the kind of challenge I loved, and I wouldn't give it up under any circumstances.

I was about to tell her that when she stood up, making a gesture of dismissal. "So if you've come here to ask me to finish Ciro's work, the answer is no. Tell that to Gabriela. I've got more valuable things to do with my time."

I got up and went to the door. "I'm sorry to hear that. With your expertise—"

"With my expertise, it would be a different book entirely. And a far better one."

As I went out, the colonel looked at me and yawned. Another tedious visitor had finally had the grace to depart.

From Mary's trailer, I walked toward the pool. The final

person I wanted to see, Sam Walters, could usually be found there. He and Gloria were a jovial couple in their seventies, and they invariably brought along a little cooler full of beer, which they shared freely with all takers. I found Sam sprawled in his usual lounge chair, a Budweiser in one hand. Aside from him, the pool area was deserted.

"Hi, Sam. Where's Gloria?" I sat down on a folding chair in the shade of a beach umbrella.

"Laundry room, earning her keep." He hooked a thumb over his shoulder and cackled loudly.

"Shame on you, you chauvinist." I'd known Sam for years and could joke as easily with him as I did with Nick.

"You want a beer?"

"Sure." I took it from his big, gnarled hand. Sam had been a construction worker until he'd retired and moved here; Gloria was his second wife, of less than ten years. "Kind of quiet today, isn't it?"

"A death and an explosion'll do that in a place like this." He took off his sunhat and wiped moisture from his bald head. "You weren't hurt, huh?"

"No. Scared, but not hurt."

"What were you doing in there?"

I was tired of the question. "Ask my mother. It was her idea."

"Already getting the estate in order, huh?"

I glanced at him to see if the remark was meant to disparage, but his expression was mild. "Sam, does everybody know Mama is Ciro's heir?"

"Most folks, I guess. He made no bones about it. Your ma did a lot of good things for him—typed manuscripts, criticized his work, reminded him when it was time to take his clothes to the cleaner. I always said that if Nick Carillo hadn't come along when he did, your ma would have been Mrs. Ciro Sisneros."

To many, the combination of a college professor and a

woman who had worked as a maid all her life would have seemed strange. But Mama, like Mary Jaramillo, was self-educated; she'd always read widely, even in those busy days when she was working and raising Carlota and me. I said, "I don't think Mama's the marrying kind."

"Maybe not. Gabriela does have a mind of her own."

"Speaking of marriage, apparently Ciro had some strong views on the subject."

Sam looked at me for a moment and then drank some beer. "You mean about mixed marriages?"

"Yes."

He glanced away, a muscle jumping in his jaw. "Yeah, he sure did. And don't think it didn't piss me off. Gloria, too. When we retired, I was all for buying a little house in a mixed neighborhood, but Glo's English isn't so good, and she wanted to be with people she could talk to. So I said I'd move here—people are just people, as far as I'm concerned. But I sure never counted on having to listen to the likes of Ciro Sisneros criticizing me next to my own swimming pool."

"What did he say?"

"The usual bullshit about cultural differences, how marriages like ours don't work out. High-and-mighty Ciro Sisneros, who'd probably never had a woman in his life." He drained the beer and crumpled the can viciously.

"Maybe he didn't mean you and Gloria specifically."

"The hell he didn't! He was looking right at us the whole time. And I know why—he was just mad because Gloria wouldn't play around with him."

"Oh, Sam—"

"No, that's true. I've seen the way he looked at her." Sam sat up and leaned toward me, his color heightened by anger. "Cultural differences—bullshit. What did Ciro know about that anyway? Glo and me, we were raised speaking two different languages, but we're as alike as can be. We both know what it's like to start with nothing, to try to build a life and then see it go down the drain again, like her first old man's and mine did in the Depression, when we were younger than you are now. Cultural differences, my ass! Ciro Sisneros had no idea, none at all, what life's really about. What right did he have to make his holler-than-thou comments? Will you explain me that, huh?"

His reddened face was close to mine, and his big gnarled hands twisted the beer can as easily as Mary Jaramillo's had crumpled the foil candy wrapper. They were strong, brutal hands and could easily have grabbed Ciro in a rage. . . .

"Sam," I said, "did you ever study judo with Ciro?"

The unexpected question quelled his anger. "Did I what?"

"Take his judo class."

"For a while, yes, but not after what he said about me and Glo. I didn't want anything to do with him—"

"Qué pasa aquí?" The voice was that of Gloria Walters, and it carried an angry edge. She was a small woman with curly black hair and a skin that was tanned to a hard, leathery texture. Gloria had the reputation of being extremely jealous of any woman who came near her Sam, and when this jealousy was inflamed, as it was now, her deep wrinkles gave her face a reptilian look.

Sam jerked back. "Nothing's going on, honey."

"What are you doing with her?" She spoke in rapid Spanish, motioning angrily at me.

"I told you, nothing."

She stood surveying us, hands on hips. "And am I supposed to believe that?"

"I tell you—"

"I *know* what you tell me. But I also know what I see."

How on earth could she be jealous of me? In Spanish, I said, "Come on, Gloria. This is Elena. The one you tried to fix your grandson up with."

"Young flesh is always sweeter." But she calmed down and took the beer Sam offered her.

"I was telling Elena about Ciro and his big speech against mixed marriages," Sam said. "I got angry, carried away."

"Ciro, that *bastardo!*" She rejected our attempt to conduct the conversation in the language she spoke most easily.

"Yes," Sam said, still in Spanish, "it was a shameful thing he did to us."

"Will you stop speaking as if I am some idiot who knows no English! Surely I have learned enough in the ten years we have been together." Then she turned to me and smiled weakly. "Adult-education classes, too. You must forgive us, Elena. These violent happenings have made everybody not themselves."

I smiled and drained my beer. "Don't worry, Gloria."

Sam offered me another Bud, but I shook my head. It was time I went to see Mama, to ask her why she hadn't told me about being Ciro's heir. Sam and Gloria both seemed relieved to see me go, and as I left them, they settled back in their chairs, looking as jovial and companionable as ever.

Gloria had said the events of the last two days had left people acting "not themselves," but I wondered. Had the upheaval actually made them, if anything, *more* themselves? And were some of those selves perhaps angry and perched dangerously on the edge of violence?

Nine

MAMA WASN'T HOME when I went to her trailer. I looked at my watch and saw that it was after three; she'd probably be at her tapestry workshop until four. The lateness of the hour gave me a twinge of conscience, so I got into my sun-heated Rabbit and drove to the museum. When I entered the parking lot, a startling sight confronted me.

Susana's little Triumph stood in the middle of the lot, entirely encased in chicken wire. Susana herself sat on the ground with Emily Hitchens, a couple of the other volunteers, and two youngish men I didn't recognize. They were surrounded by a sea of bright crepe paper, which they were busily transforming into flowers. I parked my car and went over to them.

"Qué pasa?" I asked.

Susana looked up and flushed. "Oh, Elena. I didn't think you'd be in today."

"Well, I'm here. What's that?" I gestured toward the car.

"Our float."

"Oh."

"I think I told you it is to be one of Jesse's *camaleones*."

"It looks like a sports car wrapped in chicken wire to me."

"It is only the beginning." She got up and led me over to it. "Look, here will be the dragon's head."

I looked at the oblong clump of wire that extended over the car's hood. I nodded dubiously.

"And the rest is the bird's body."

Jesse's papier-mâché animals combined various forms into one body, with surprising and often graceful results. I knew the one that this was supposedly modeled on, and I didn't see how they were going to achieve any similarity. "What are you going to do, stuff those paper flowers through the chicken wire?" I asked.

"Yes. Like they do for the Rose Bowl Parade, only with fake flowers instead of real ones."

"Oh."

"Elena, you seem displeased."

"No, I'm looking forward to seeing it. You *are* going to leave holes so the driver can see where he's going?"

"It is all planned."

"Well, good." I turned to go inside, then stopped. "Who's answering the phones and watching the galleries while you're creating this . . . creation?" I'd almost said "monstrosity."

"There are other volunteers in the galleries. And Linda has said she will take telephone messages."

Linda Trujillo was our education director and presumably had better things to attend to than answering the phone—namely, the production of our new catalog. "How long is it going to take to build the float?" I asked.

"We will work all night until it is finished."

"Good. Then everyone will be back at his job tomorrow."

"Yes, Elena," Susana said with a faintly exasperated inflection.

When I turned back toward the museum, Jesse Herrera was coming through the loading-dock door with a six-pack in his hand. He was a handsome young man with unruly black hair and bright shoe-button eyes. He waved merrily when he saw me, then began distributing beer to the workers. I waited until he was done, then motioned to him.

"Are you sure this thing is going to work?" I asked.

Susana heard me and looked up, her eyes flashing.

Jesse shrugged. "Reasonably. I helped build one for homecoming in high school and it didn't fall apart."

"It had better not. All we need to improve our image is a float that collapses in the middle of State Street Saturday night."

"Don't worry, *amiga*. It's all in my capable hands." He held them out, flexing his lean artist's fingers. "I will even drive, to make sure all goes well."

"Thanks." I studied Jesse, noting the dark circles under his eyes. His outward manner might be light and cheery, but I knew he'd had bad nights lately and wasn't working too well. Jesse was getting over a love affair that had gone sour. "By the way," I said, "I meant to get up to see your grandmother about those paintings before this, but I've had personal problems."

"*Pobrecita*. Do you want to tell me about them? You've certainly listened to enough of mine recently."

"Actually, I do. Let's go to my office."

Jesse turned to the group on the ground. "I want those flowers done by the time I get back. And no messing with the girls, Walt."

One of the young men looked up and flashed us a grin. "Friends from my apartment complex," Jesse explained to me. "They're in between sessions at City College and bored enough to be talked into such a project."

We went inside to my office, Jesse stopping in the kitchen to get us beers. He listened quietly as I told him about Ciro's murder and the few things I'd found out. "Obviously," I added, "there was something important in Ciro's research materials. I can roughly remember the time spans missing from his notes, but I don't know enough about local history to fill in the gaps."

Jesse looked thoughtful. "You say the book was to be on the Great Depression?"

"Yes."

"What were some of those dates?"

"Nineteen thirty-five comes to mind. Almost the whole year, but particularly August. Thirty-four, some of it, but I don't know what months. It's not much to go on."

"Not unless you know an authority on local history."

"Well, Mary Jaramillo is one, but I don't think she'd help me. Besides, she's one of the people who may have killed Ciro. Probably the best suspect, since her anger with him is connected to his work, as was the threat he received."

"Ah, but she is not the only authority." Jesse smiled triumphantly. "I know another, a lady who lived through those years and has the memory of an elephant."

"Who's that?"

"My grandmother."

"Is this a ploy to get me to go to Ojai and see those paintings? I really do intend to go."

"Then go right away. You will be accomplishing two tasks at once. Abuela Felicia will be able to tell you everything you want to know, and more. She loves to talk."

"In that case, I'll do it. Will it be all right if I just show up, since she doesn't have a phone?"

"Guests are welcome at any time, any day. She's lonely, and I must confess I don't get up there as often as I should. I'll draw you a map of how to get to her place." He reached for a piece of scratch paper and sketched quickly.

I pocketed the paper, and we went back out to the parking lot. The flowers weren't finished yet, but there were a lot more of them.

As I started for my car, Susana called, "Elena, you are not leaving?"

"Yes. I'm on my way to Ojai, to see Jesse's grandmother."

"It is about time."

I made a face at her.

Emily Hitchens suddenly dumped the crepe-paper flowers from her lap and stood up. "Elena, can I go with you?"

I hesitated.

"You said it would be good to have company on the drive."

Her face was so eager that I couldn't say no. "All right, come on along."

Susana began to protest at losing one of her workers, but Jesse silenced her by saying, "I'll go back to my apartment complex and round up more volunteers when people get home from work."

Mollified, she went back to fashioning flowers. Emily and I got into the car and left.

She was silent as I drove across town to Route 101, watching the passing streets as intently as if they were new to her. Finally, as I turned south on the highway, I said, "Where do you live, Emily? Here in town?"

"Yes, we have a studio, actually. The landlady's in her eighties and can't get around so well, so she gives me cheap rent in exchange for running her errands."

"We?"

She hesitated. "I meant my cat and me."

"Oh, she lets you have a cat. That's nice; most landlords won't, you know."

"Yes, it's a very good deal." She looked over at me, her face set in polite lines, like a person who is bored but pretending to have a good time at a cocktail party. "Do you have any pets?"

"No. I suppose if a stray cat were to come around, I'd let it move in. But it would probably work out badly. I haven't been very good with living things these last few years. Even my houseplants have to be cacti—except for some African violets my mother left when she moved out. *They* just keep on and on, in spite of the fact that I hate them and have done everything possible to kill them. I call them my 'African violence.' "

Emily apparently didn't see the humor in it. "Why don't you give them away if you hate them?"

"I don't know. I never thought of it." Then I was silent

until I made the turn onto Casitas Pass Road, brooding a little about not being good with plants or pets. Actually, I wasn't much good with people either recently. At the museum I was always rushed and short-tempered; when I went home, I holed up and sometimes didn't answer the phone. The only person I knew who remotely approached being a boyfriend was Carlos, and I didn't fit into his world—or want to.

"Do you have a boyfriend, Emily?"

She looked mildly surprised at such a personal question but said, "No. Santa Barbara seems to be full of three-piecers, and that's not my type."

"Mine either."

Again she seemed to feel obligated to make conversation. "Are you seeing anybody?"

"Only Carlos Bautista, and that relationship's kind of tepid."

"The board chairman?"

"Yes. He's a nice man, and rich as can be, but no more my type than the fellows who hang out in the fern bars."

"He *is* nice." She looked thoughtful, then added, "I'll bet you Susana would give a lot to be in your shoes."

"Oh?"

"Yes, Carlos was at the museum earlier—looking for you, I think. Susana was flirting, hanging on every word he said."

I felt a prickle of annoyance. *"Por Dios,* Susana is seventeen years old. What does she want with Carlos?"

"Susana is a good deal older than her years." Emily paused, her pale face anxious. "Elena, I don't know if I should talk this way to you, but ... if I were you, I'd watch out for Susana. She's extremely ambitious."

I thought of the dream I'd had of Carlos and Susana standing across the fountain from me, their arms around one another, laughing. "I know what you mean. And thanks for the warning."

"Well, I didn't know if I should say anything or not."

"I'm glad you did."

We were silent once more as we crossed the pass road and dropped down into the moon-shaped Ojai Valley, nestled within the protecting arms of the Topa and Sulphur mountain chains. The land was dotted with orchards and streams, and horses and cattle grazed on the hillsides. When the road wound past Lake Casitas, I could see rowboats full of fishermen and the bright colors of tents in the campgrounds, and not long after that we drove into Ojai.

The town is an artists' colony, and parts of it are very little changed from the old Spanish days. Known for its cultural activities, Ojai sponsors a music festival every May and a folk-dance festival every other year, as well as "art Sundays," which are extremely profitable for resident artists. Emily stared out the window with real interest now as we drove down the main street past an old Spanish shopping arcade with a facade of arches and a bell tower.

"Does Jesse's grandmother live right here in town?" she asked.

"No, on a ranch in the hills about ten miles southeast of here. Apparently, she worked for the rancher for many years, and when she retired, he deeded her a small house on the property."

"And these paintings—they depict the farm labor struggle?"

"Yes. From what Jesse told me, some of them go all the way back to the thirties, the time that Steinbeck was writing about in *The Grapes of Wrath*. Others are more modern, almost up to the present day."

"Are they watercolors?"

"Yes."

"And did she do them all?"

"I think she did only some of them. Abuela—grand-mother—Felicia was active in the labor struggle when she first came to California from Mexico, so the early ones are probably hers. But later her eyesight went. According to Jesse, she continued to collect the paintings as a hobby."

"I thought Jesse said she was poor. How could she afford them?"

I shrugged. "Maybe they were given to her. She still has many friends in the labor movement. I only know she wants to sell them because she needs money badly."

I turned onto the side road indicated on Jesse's map. It wound up into the hills, dipping down into canyons filled with scrub oak. It was almost seven o'clock, and although it had been daylight when we'd passed through Ojai, the thick vegetation here in the higher hills created a murky twilight. We passed no other cars, and I felt a sudden sense of relief at having Emily along with me. When we came to the stone arches guarding the entrance to the ranch, I almost drove by them.

The adobe ranch house stood straight ahead, dark, with its windows shuttered. "It looks abandoned," Emily said in a hushed voice.

"I think the owners have died or retired somewhere else. Jesse once mentioned that Abuela Felicia lives in a lonely place."

I guided the car around the big house, as Jesse's map indicated, and down a rutted drive toward the outbuildings in the distance. The thickly forested hills loomed dark behind them, and the shapes of the buildings were blurred in the shadows.

Emily shivered. "How can she stand it out here?"

"Well, she's lived here most of her life. Some people like solitude." I had always considered myself one of those people, preferring to withdraw into the quiet of my little house after battling with the world all day. But at home there were cries of children from the street, the occasional sound of traffic, noise from neighbors' radios and TVs. Here there was nothing but silence and the infrequent calls of nocturnal birds. For Emily's sake, however, I controlled the urge to shiver too.

To our left was a barn with an empty corral and some sheds. Straight ahead, in a grove of eucalyptus trees, was a small adobe cottage, built on the style of the big house. Dim light shone in its windows. I pulled the car up about ten yards away from it and said, "This must be it."

Emily sat still, looking first at the cottage and then around at the thick oak and eucalyptus groves. "Are you sure?"

"Of course." I opened the door and got out of the car. "Come on, you're acting like a city slicker, letting the silence spook you."

At that moment, said silence was broken by a mournful cry from the direction of the dark barn. Emily's hand flew to her mouth. "What was that?"

"Probably an owl. Come *on*."

She smiled weakly and got out.

As we turned toward the cottage, a shape appeared in its door, silhouetted against the light inside. It was a small, stooped figure dressed in black. It raised its hand and beckoned to us. I gave Emily a little shove, and we started forward.

Ten

JESSE'S ABUELA FELICIA had wrinkled features and pale gray hair, but her bright eyes were as alive as her grandson's. Right now they sparkled at the sight of Emily and me.

"You must be Elena Oliverez," she said in a surprisingly deep voice. "Jesus wrote me that you would come."

"I'm sorry it took so long. This is one of our museum volunteers, Emily Hitchens."

Abuela Felicia smiled at Emily—who stood a little behind me, her arms crossed over her breasts—then turned and motioned for us to follow her inside. "It did not take you so very long, and I am delighted you have arrived. Out here, every day is more or less like the others, and to have company is always a pleasure."

We entered a room that was lighted by a fire on a small stone hearth and a pink lamp whose base was a sculpture of a nymph holding a tambourine. The furniture was old but comfortable-looking, probably purchased secondhand or cast off from the ranch house. A television was showing the evening news, but Abuela Felicia turned it off and motioned for us to sit on the couch.

"I hope the fire does not make it too warm for you," she said. "At my age one can never get warm enough. And now may I offer you some coffee? I have a nice South American blend that Jesus brings me."

We both accepted, and Abuela Felicia left the room, walking slowly.

Emily looked around. "I don't see the paintings."

"We'll get to them. First we must spend some time socializing. She's lonely."

"Of course."

We lapsed into silence, listening to noises from what must be the kitchen. In a few minutes, Jesse's grandmother returned with a coffeepot. As if to apologize for her earlier impatience, Emily jumped up and helped her clear a space on the low oak table. Abuela Felicia went back to the kitchen for cups, cream, and sugar. She poured and served as if she were entertaining in a grand hacienda, rather than a caretaker's cottage.

"And how is my grandson?" she asked when she was settled in a platform rocker close to the fire.

"He's fine," I said. "Tonight he's building a float for the Fiesta parade—it's modeled after one of his *camaleones.*"

"Ah, es muy bueno." She looked at Emily. "Do you speak Spanish?"

"*Sí.*"

I glanced at her in surprise. It was not an ability that she had mentioned when she'd volunteered at the museum.

"Then we will talk in Spanish," Abuela Felicia said in that language. "I learned English shortly after I came to this country, but as I grow older, I forget more and more of it. Jesus has told you about the paintings?"

"Yes. They sound like something the museum would be interested in acquiring. Of course I'll have to appraise them and then get the approval of our board of directors—"

She dismissed the complexities with a wave of her hand. "That is fine. If you like, you may take them with you tonight. I trust my grandson's friends as I trust him, even if he is very remiss about coming to visit me." Her eyes twinkled merrily.

"But first," she went on, "I must ask you: Has Jesus gotten over this disappointment in love?"

"I think he's mending."

"It was a sad thing, but for the best. Now he is free to find someone who will really care for him." She gave me a long, speculative look, and for a moment I was reminded of my mother.

"Abuela Felicia—if I may call you that?" I said.

She nodded.

"Jesse told me you might be able to help me with some questions I have, questions about things that happened during the Great Depression."

"I will try."

Next to me, Emily shifted impatiently. Why this hurry to get the paintings and leave? I wondered. Surely the isolation of the ranch couldn't have disturbed her that much.

"The Great Depression covered many years, child," the old woman said. "Which of those in particular are you interested in?"

"Probably nineteen thirty-five. But I can't say for certain." Briefly I told her about Ciro's death and the documents that had been stolen from his files.

When I had finished, Abuela Felicia looked off into the fire. "Nineteen thirty-five," she said, and then fell silent.

I waited. Even Emily seemed to have forgotten her impatience; she set down her coffee cup and leaned forward, watching the old woman.

After a few moments, Abuela Felicia spoke. "You say, in particular, August of nineteen thirty-five?"

"Yes."

"Then what you are looking for is probably the legend of the slain soldiers."

"The legend of the slain soldiers . . . I heard something about that only the other night. It is a fiesta, is it not—to commemorate *La Raza*?"

She shook her head. "Not exactly. It is a fiesta, yes. And it is celebrated more and more now, as times grow harder.

But it does not commemorate the modern struggle. It goes back further—to the evil times during the Depression."

In the thirties, she told us, great controversy had raged in the fields of California's San Joaquin Valley near Bakersfield. The agricultural workers were organizing to strike against the landowners. But within the labor movement itself there was also dissension.

"At that time there were many who emigrated to California from other parts of the country," Abuela Felicia explained. "Through the false advertising of those landowners who sought cheap labor, the state had acquired a reputation as a land of plenty. Those who came here were mainly from the central part of the United States, where they had been forced off their land by greedy corporations. They had suffered drought at home and terrible deprivations on their journey west. And when they arrived, they faced great disappointment. Work was scarce, and when it could be found, it was back-breaking labor. All their money went for food and shelter. Ah, well, you know your history." She paused. "Of course, most of those who came then were Anglos."

"And then there were those like you," I said.

"Yes, there were those like me who had come from Mexico earlier and had begun to make a life for themselves. When these Anglos came streaming in, they threatened that life. It was a difficult time, and as difficult times are, it was without honor."

At first, she explained, the newly formed unions had tried to make the factions work together peaceably. But the leaders, generally imported from other parts of the country and insensitive to local tensions, could not mend the schism which had arisen. In August 1935, a great strike was mounted against a group of Bakersfield-area lettuce growers. The workers, primarily Mexican-Americans, walked out, determined to fight for a living wage. But the growers took advantage of the newly arrived Anglos and hired many of them as scabs.

"One cannot blame the scabs," Abuela Felicia said. "They were desperate, down to their last scraps of food. They had left behind most of the things they cared about and sold the others along the way, to put food in their children's bellies. But our people naturally resented them."

"The Mexican-American faction in the union was led by Alberto Ortega, a descendant of the family that once held the land grant for Refugio Beach—you know that place above Santa Barbara which is now a state park?"

I nodded, then glanced at Emily. She sat, her hands clasped together, her lips slightly parted.

"Alberto Ortega had his faults," Jesse's grandmother went on, "but he was a strong leader, and with two of his closest friends he was able to bring our people together in a way that no one but Chavez has since. He organized the strike and convinced the people to risk all and walk out. And then, when we did, the Anglos walked in—into our jobs, our fields, even into the shacks the growers had provided for us."

Emily cleared her throat. "It sounds as if you were there." Her voice trembled with some indefinable emotion.

Abuela Felicia glanced at her curiously, then studied her face for a moment. "I was, child. One of the shacks usurped by the Anglos—Okies, they called them then—was the home my husband and I shared with Jesus's mother and our five other children."

Emily looked down at her clasped hands, her hair falling limply across her cheek. One of the logs in the fireplace broke, crashing to the grate and sending out a shower of sparks, but she didn't seem to notice.

Abuela Felicia went on. "What happened, of course, was inevitable. The pickets attacked the scabs. Armed combat broke out. There was a shooting, and the son of one of the growers died. Alberto Ortega was accused—conveniently—of the murder, and he and his two friends fled the valley."

"Where did they go?" I asked.

"Refugio Beach, where the original Ortega rancho was. The family had not owned the land for many years, but Alberto was familiar with the terrain and doubtless thought it a good place to hide. They camped there two nights, awaiting word from the valley. On the morning of the third day, a messenger from the union came to tell them Alberto had been exonerated of the killing; a minor union official had confessed to shooting the grower's son by accident."

I had a sudden sense of foreboding—strange to feel that way about something long in the past. Emily must have felt it too, because she looked up, her eyes wide in the flickering firelight.

"But?" I said.

"But when the union messenger arrived, Alberto Ortega and his friends were dead. Shot to death beside their campfire. It was an irony for someone to end Alberto's life on the land formerly belonging to his family, no?"

I was silent for a moment. "Did they ever find out who shot them?"

"A medallion that Alberto always wore around his neck as a symbol of the cause had been ripped from his body. Because of that, it has always been assumed that he and his companions were killed by the growers or a rival faction in the labor union. The deaths were called a martyrdom and for years were celebrated as the Fiesta of the Slain Soldiers."

There had been an odd inflection in her voice when she said, "it has always been assumed." I said, "Do you believe that's the answer to who killed them?"

She shook her head slowly. "I am old, child, and my memory fails me, who am I to say?"

Emily said, "The fiesta, it's celebrated even now, isn't it?"

"Yes. For many years, especially in the thirties, it was a rallying time for the labor movement. Then, with the coming of the war, our concerns were elsewhere. In the first days of Chavez, it was revived somewhat, but the leaders of that time wanted their own heroes, rather than giving the honor to men so long dead. Now, because we are once more losing ground, the fiesta is back again."

"Isn't there something else about it?" Emily asked. "A love story?"

I turned to look at her. She was full of surprises—first knowing Spanish, and now having information about one of our people's legends that I'd only heard of two days before.

Seeing that I'd turned my head, she said, "I'm from a farming community, Elena. Some of our workers were Mexican-American."

Of course, I thought. Lindsay, where the olives are grown.

Abuela Felicia's face had softened. "Yes, there is a love story, a tragic one. Alberto Ortega had been said to have a bad way with women for many years; he had been involved with the daughter of a fellow labor organizer—a girl of unsavory reputation whom he had gotten into trouble and then forced to have an abortion. But while organizing the strike, he met and fell in love with a good woman, the daughter of an Italian landowner. It was said that their union would forge a greater understanding between the workers and the growers, the Anglos and our people."

"What happened to her?" I asked.

Abuela Felicia stared into the fire. "She went on. For several years she went on. But then one day, on the anniversary of Ortega's death, she went to Refugio Beach and walked into the sea. She loved him that much."

In spite of the control and sophistication I like to think I possess, tears sprang to my eyes, and I, too, looked into the flames. "I don't think I'll ever love anyone that much."

The old woman said, "It is rare, and a gift of God."

We sat watching the fire for a long time. There were tears in Emily's eyes too, and she had obviously forgotten all about the paintings. Finally Abuela Felicia said, "Does this help you, Elena?"

"Yes, it does. I know now that the material removed from Ciro Sisneros's files has to be that on the legend of the slain soldiers."

"And what will you do with this knowledge?"

"Of that I'm not certain. Not certain at all." Then I looked at my watch and realized we should collect the paintings and get back to town. When I said so, the old woman led us to a storeroom and showed us where they were. There were thirty, and it took a good fifteen minutes for Emily and me to wrap them securely in some old blankets and load them into the back of my car. Declining Abuela Felicia's offer of another cup of coffee, we thanked her and headed back toward Santa Barbara.

All the way back to town, Emily and I didn't speak. I felt as if I were half in the present and half back in the distant world Abuela Felicia had described to us. It was a time when life was harder but somehow fuller; a time when men and women had cared deeply enough to die for honor—or for love.

I glanced at Emily a few times, but she was staring out at the darkness. Once I saw her raise her hand and surreptitiously wipe at her eyes. Was she crying? I wondered. For whom? Alberto Ortega and his love? Or for something more immediate and personal?

When we got to the museum, however, there were no signs of tears on her face. And when I told her we'd have to remove the paintings from the car and haul them down to the basement storage room before I could drive her home, she made no objection. That in itself surprised me; it was after eleven, and the prospect of the task made me weary.

Cursing because the float—now covered in plastic drop-cloths—blocked the space in front of the loading dock, I eased the car around it and stopped. When I got out, I went over and tried to peek under the plastic, but it was securely fastened down. It was probably just as well, I thought—it would only disturb my sleep if the thing looked as horrible as I imagined. I went back to the car, unlocked the hatchback, and Emily and I piled the paintings on the loading dock. Then I turned off the alarm system, unlocked the door, and we moved them inside and downstairs.

For a couple of months after we'd moved into the old adobe, the basement had been a jumble of packing cases and old furniture. But now it was organized, with new shelves and a large central work table. I'd even persuaded the board to okay the purchase of fluorescent lights with ultraviolet shields. Emily and I piled the paintings on the work table, went up for more, and finally we were finished.

Sighing, I leaned against the shelf behind me. "Well, that's done."

"Yes. Can we look at the paintings now?" Each had been encased in thick layers of brown paper—presumably the way Abuela Felicia had kept them stored for years—in addition to the blankets we'd borrowed to cushion them on the ride.

"Sure." In spite of the late hour, I was curious too.

She unwrapped one and looked at it, then handed it to me. It was from the thirties, showing workers—a family with small children—in an orchard. "This is good," I said. "Very good."

Emily handed me another, depicting a long line of laborers in a field that stretched endlessly toward the sunbrowned mountains. "We could make a wonderful display with these—" I began.

Emily made a sighing sound, and I glanced anxiously at her. She wavered, and then her knees buckled and she slipped toward the floor. I managed to catch her by the shoulders, then lowered her the rest of the way. She lay there, her eyes closed, her head lolling over onto her right shoulder.

Fearfully, I grabbed her wrist and felt for her pulse but found none. I was about to run upstairs to call the paramedics when I realized I was feeling with my thumb; my own pulse was canceling out hers. Dropping her wrist, I put my hand to her neck and felt the throb of her artery. It was strong and regular; apparently she'd merely fainted.

Now what? How did you revive someone who had fainted? Movies always showed people with smelling salts, chafing at the unconscious heroine's cold hands. Somehow that didn't seem appropriate in this situation.

Emily groaned. Her eyelids fluttered and she looked up at me. "Oh," she said.

"Are you okay?"

"Oh." She moved her head from side to side and then tried to sit up.

I pushed her back. "Just lie still for a minute. I don't want you passing out again."

She raised her arm and covered her eyes with the crook of her elbow. "I guess . . . it must have happened because I didn't eat dinner."

It was true we hadn't bothered to eat. But fainting like this . . . I hadn't eaten many a time, but it had never caused me to pass out. "Are you sure that's all it is? Has this happened before?"

"Never." She sat up, shaking out her pale hair. "Really, Elena, I'm okay."

But now I was worried about her. She didn't have a job, and she'd said she was living on some money she had saved. Maybe she was trying to conserve those funds and was eating poorly. Right then, seeing her looking greenish and sick under the bright fluorescent lights, I decided to make getting Emily Hitchens gainful employment one of my top priorities.

"Come on," I said, holding out my hand. "Let's lock up and get you home."

She let me help her up, then turned and began smoothing the blanket back over a painting of a modern picket line. As she went to rewrap the others, I said, "Leave those. They'll be okay overnight."

She nodded and dutifully followed me toward the stairs. We went through the silent museum and out to the parking lot. The float stood there, like a giant chrysalis ready to spawn some horrible bug instead of a butterfly. I looked at it and shuddered.

When I turned to Emily, she was standing still, staring at the plastic-wrapped float as if the awful bug were already emerging. "Come on," I repeated gently, "it's time to go home."

Eleven

WHEN I DROVE into the museum parking lot Thursday morning, the giant insect had emerged from its cocoon, and it was indeed the ugliest bug I'd ever laid eyes on. Apparently the dampness of the night air had gotten to it, and the colors of the crepe-paper flowers—formerly the national red, green, and white of Mexico—had run together into a disgusting brown. The flowers themselves drooped dispiritedly, ready to be plowed under to make way for next year's crop.

And it looked like another crop was just what Susana had in mind. She had two of the volunteers plucking blossoms from the chicken wire, and three more sat on the ground fashioning fresh ones. Susana herself ran back and forth, giving instructions. When she saw me getting out of my car, she stood still, a sheepish expression on her face.

"You have a little problem here?" I said, motioning at the float.

"It is not necessary to rub it in, Elena."

"So what's all this—you're going to redo it?"

"Yes. The . . . the thing Jesse calls 'the concept' is still good."

"That's true, but now I have another concept for you: This is a museum, not a high school preparing for the homecoming parade. There are phones to be answered and letters to be typed. There are galleries to be tended and visitors' questions to be answered. In short, we have no more time for the float."

Her finely penciled eyebrows drew together. "Elena, you are not thinking in terms of public relations."

"That's also true. I am only thinking in terms of keeping this establishment running so we can serve the public. This is Fiesta; the place is overrun with tourists. We must be available to help them—and to make sure they don't damage the artworks."

A look of fury crossed her small face, and I remembered Emily's warning of the night before. I also remembered a different Susana—the one who had aided her thieving husband in a scheme that had almost destroyed the museum. Out of kindness, because she had been young and in love, I'd chosen to forget that other Susana, but now I wasn't so sure that had been the right decision.

"Also," I said, "if you rebuild the float today, the same thing will happen to the flowers tonight. If you're going to do it at all, do it on the day of the parade."

"But that is when we must get ready for the fiestas!"

"It doesn't take all day to dress for a party. Do it then, or not at all."

As I started down the path to the courtyard entrance to my office, I heard Susana say, "Elena, she is like the *osa negra*!"

I smiled, in spite of my annoyance. "Black bear" described my mood better than she knew.

Susana obeyed my instructions, however. All morning the phones were answered on the first ring, and I could hear her typewriter clacking away outside my office. I made a few trips through the galleries, to make sure they—and the ever-increasing crowds of visitors—were being properly supervised. Otherwise I spent the time going over the printing estimate for our new catalog and conferring with Linda Trujillo about the copy for it. By eleven-thirty, when the phone rang and a sullen Susana announced a call from Carlos Bautista, I was feeling I'd accomplished a good morning's work.

"Elena," Carlos's deep voice said when I picked up the receiver, "I have been trying to reach you."

"Yes, I heard you were here yesterday. I'm sorry I missed you."

"No more sorry than I."

"Was there something important you needed to see me about?"

"No, I just wished to talk."

Talk about what? The disaster of a date we'd had the other night? To forestall such a discussion, I said, "Carlos, I have good news. Do you remember those labor-movement paintings that Jesse Herrera's grandmother has for sale? I think I mentioned them."

"Yes, of course. We discussed whether they were compatible with the original aims of the museum."

"And I believe you said I was free to take a new direction if I thought it wise."

"Yes."

"Well, I went to Ojai and got the paintings last night. From the couple I looked at, I think they're very good. Of course I have to appraise them—and I'm hoping to get to that this afternoon—but I think they're just what we need to put together a showing that reflects the Mexican-American community and its history here in the area."

"That's good, very good. You'll get back to me when you have a figure, so I can take it up with the board?"

"Certainly." I tried to think of some other topic to distract him from the personal. "Also, Carlos, there's a volunteer here, Emily Hitchens, who looks very promising. I'd like to give her a paying position, even if it's only parttime."

"What kind of position?"

"I'm not sure. But her abilities are far superior to the type of volunteer we usually attract—"

"Hitchens. That's an Anglo name."

"Yes, but she speaks Spanish fluently. And she seems to know and care a great deal about our history and traditions."

"See what you can find for her then. And again, let me know."

"I will. But now I must go—"

"Elena, I called for another reason besides paintings and volunteers."

Here it came. "Yes, Carlos."

"I would like to ask you to a party on Saturday night."

"A party."

"Yes. A dinner party in honor of the end of Fiesta week."

"Oh."

"Elena, are you so wrapped up in your work that you can't look forward to a party?"

"It's not that, Carlos." Now what was I to do? I could plead a previous engagement, but Carlos knew me well enough to realize I hardly ever made plans in advance. And I wasn't a good enough liar to succeed anyway. Also, I remembered Emily's warning: "Susana was hanging on every word Carlos said. . . . She's extremely ambitious." And then I thought of my dream—the two of them standing together across the fountain, laughing at me. Was Carlos petty enough to retaliate because of a personal rejection? Retaliate by making my job more difficult—or taking it away altogether?

"Elena?"

"Yes, I'm here. I was just checking my calendar. I'd love to go to a party with you."

We set a time, and I hung up, feeling as if I'd just sold my soul. And I couldn't fool myself by claiming that was sexual harassment—after all, *I* was the one who had imposed the necessity for the date upon myself. I sat at my desk, staring at the marked-up copy for the new catalog, feeling lower and lower. I'd just about hit rock bottom when the intercom buzzed and Susana—still sullen—announced Lieutenant Dave Kirk on line one.

My spirits rose considerably. Maybe he'd take me to lunch again and cheer me with talk of the investigation. I smiled as I picked up the receiver, thinking: What sort of woman gets cheered up by talking about murder?

But Kirk didn't want to see me. Instead, he was all business. "Elena," he said, "I need your help."

"How?"

"It's that old witch at the trailer park."

"Adela Hernandez?"

"Yes. I contacted her again this morning about getting that list of the people who were on the chartered bus trip to El Mercado, plus the roster of students in Ciro Sisneros's judo classes. She claims she's too busy to compile them."

"Did you tell her she's obstructing a police investigation?"

He made an irritated sound. "Of course I did. But I can only push so far, unless I want to lose cooperation from all the people at the park. I wonder if you'd go up there and talk her out of the information."

I paused. It would get me out of here, give me time to think about whether I really wanted to keep that date with Carlos. And Adela, for all her carping and criticism, really did like me; I could probably accomplish what Kirk was asking. "All right. But you'll owe me something for this."

"What?"

"I don't know. A beer. Another burrito."

"I think we can do better than that."

I hung up, surprised. When he'd said those last words, Kirk's voice had modulated to a teasing softness I'd never heard him use before. Maybe my mother had been right all along; maybe this unreadable Anglo did like me. But I'd previously been involved with several Anglos; was I interested in a relationship with another? One more thing to consider, along with my feelings toward Carlos Bautista.

Adela Hernandez was cleaning the swimming pool when I arrived at the trailer park. She stood in the shallow end, wielding a long-handled vacuum cleaner, clad in an old-fashioned black bathing suit with a flouncy skirt. In spite of being in the water, beads of sweat stood out on her bony shoulders. It was the hottest part of the day and only diehard sunbathers— the Walters couple and two women I didn't know—had ventured out to the pool area.

When I stopped at the edge of the pool, Adela looked up at me, shading her eyes with one hand. "You again," she said.

"Me again," I acknowledged cheerfully.

"I suppose that Anglo cop sent you."

"Yes, he did." I sat down, took off one sandal, and stuck my foot in the water.

"Don't do that," Adela said. "I'm cleaning."

I didn't see what difference it made, but I removed my foot. "Can we talk?"

"In a few minutes. I'm almost done." She turned her back and went on vacuuming the pool's bottom.

I retreated to a lounge chair in the shade and watched her. She moved the vacuum through the water with strong, steady strokes, never missing an inch of the cement surface. I wondered why the trailer park's owners didn't employ a pool-cleaning service, then decided Adela probably enjoyed doing it. She was a vigorous woman, and other than pool cleaning her job didn't permit her to get much exercise. Besides, having to perform such a menial task gave her something else to complain about.

When Adela climbed dripping from the pool, she snatched up a towel from a nearby chair and motioned curtly at me. I followed her wet footprints across the cement to the rec center and through there to her office.

"Wait here," she said, and went into her apartment. In a few minutes she returned, swathed in a white terry-cloth robe. 'Now, what is it?"

"Dave Kirk says he asked you for a list of the people who were in Ciro's judo class and also of those who went on the bus trip to El Mercado. You refused to give them to him."

"Oh, so it's 'Dave,' not 'Lieutenant Kirk.' Is he another of your Anglo boyfriends?"

"Adela—"

"And I did not refuse to give them to him, I said I'd get to it when I could."

"It would only take a couple of minutes. You could have done it while he was here."

She scowled. "A lot you know about my job. You have no idea how hard it is to keep this place running properly. But why would you? Here you are, at one in the afternoon, able to just run off from that fancy office of yours anytime it suits you—"

The door behind me opened, and I glanced over my shoulder. Joe Garcia stood there.

"That's the last of it," he said, motioning toward the front of the building. "and here are the keys."

Adela reached out and took the keychain he was extending.

"We're all square now?" Garcia asked, looking directly at Adela, as if I weren't there.

"Unless I find you've trashed the place," she said.

Garcia flushed. "You won't find nothing of the kind."

"Good. Because if I do, I know where to find you."

The little man stood quivering with indignation. Finally he muttered, "Bitchy as ever, ain't you?" and turned toward the door.

"Adela," I said, "is he moving out?"

"Yes, and good riddance to him."

"Did he leave a forwarding address?"

"Of course."

I turned and watched Garcia cross the lobby of the rec center. He was one of Dave Kirk's suspects, and his moving so soon after Ciro's murder made him seem even more suspicious. If Garcia had killed Ciro, he had probably given Adela a false forwarding address.

I ran out of the rec center, following Garcia across the lawn to the parking lot, where a car with a U-Haul trailer stood.

"Mr. Garcia, wait!" I called. "Please wait."

He turned, annoyance plain on his face.

I ran up to him. "Why are you moving?"

"What business is that of yours?"

It wasn't my business at all, and I couldn't think of an answer. "Well," I said lamely, "it's so soon after Ciro's death."

"What's Ciro's death got to do with me?"

"Well—"

"Look, young lady, I know you've played detective before, but if you're doing that again, you can leave me alone. Nobody told me to stay in town. Nobody said they thought I had anything to do with what happened to Sisneros. I go where I want, when I want. And I don't have to answer to the likes of you. So butt out." Then he went to the car with the U-Haul, started it up, and drove slowly out of the lot.

I couldn't see the license plate of his car, but I could see the one on the trailer. I copied it down on one of the blank checks from my purse, then ran back to the office.

"Adela," I said, "what forwarding address did Joe Garcia give you?"

She let out a long-suffering sigh but looked it up in a card file. "It's a post-office box. Number eleven-forty-two, in Los Angeles."

"Zip code?"

"He didn't know it."

That sounded suspicious. Given the efficiency of the postal service, no letter would ever get to Garcia at a post-office box with no zip code. In fact, there probably wasn't any box with such a low number in that huge metropolis; Garcia might as well have specified General Delivery.

"Can I use the phone?"

She motioned wearily. "Go ahead."

I picked up the receiver and dialed the sheriff's department. Dave Kirk, of course, wasn't in. I slammed the receiver down and then realized Adela was holding out a sheet of paper to me.

"What's this?" I asked.

"The lists you want. It's the only way to get rid of you."

I took the sheet and looked it over. On the top half she'd listed the people who had taken the bus trip to El Mercado. Joe Garcia's name wasn't there, nor was Mary Jaramillo's. Gloria Walters had gone, but not Sam. Odd, I thought. The Walters couple did everything together.

On the bottom of the page was a shorter list, the roster of Ciro's judo classes. Sam Walters had taken from him, but not his wife or Garcia or Mary. I studied the names a little longer, noting Nick's, as well as many of his friends, the close-knit group of late-blooming athletes to whom he referred affectionately as his "old fogeys." It was hard to imagine any of them killing anyone, much less Ciro. Besides, the killer didn't necessarily have to have studied judo with Ciro; classes were given all over, in every city and town in the country.

I looked at the lists and sighed, realizing they were next to useless.

Adela made an impatient sound. "Is that all, Elena?"

"Oh. Oh, yes. Thank you for your help."

"You should have been a cop."

"What?"

"A cop."

"Why?"

"Because you are very persistent—and annoying."

I took that as my dismissal and left without retorting. It

was funny about Adela; she could say the most awful thing
to people, but they hardly ever retaliated.

I had been planning to go right back to work, but I decided
to stop by my mother's trailer on the off chance she might be
home. And for once she was—in the kitchen making tortillas.

"What's all this about?" I asked. "Are you still planning
to have the party on Saturday?" When Mama had retired to
the trailer park, she'd decided to take what she called a "true
retirement." That meant that everything didn't have to be
homemade. The tortilla-making, once a weekly ritual in our
house, was now reserved for special occasions.

She pinched off some of the whitish dough and rolled it
into a ball. "Yes, in spite of Ciro's death we have decided not
to cancel it. People need to cheer up. I am in charge of the
tortillas, and this afternoon I am getting a head start on it."

"They won't be very fresh."

She gave me one of her dark looks. "And what would you
know about that? I bet you buy your tortillas at Safeway."

"Well . . ."

"Besides, no one will notice. It is a fiesta, and the beer and
margaritas will flow. Alcohol dulls the tastebuds." In spite of
her censorious tone, I knew Mama was looking forward to
the party. And she enjoyed a few drinks as much as anybody
else in the park.

"Can I help?"

"There is no tortilla press in this house." She began patting
the little ball of dough, and as if it had a life of its own, it
assumed the proper round shape.

"It's not my fault I never learned to make tortillas by hand.
You never let Carlota and me help out in the kitchen."

"There were better things for you to do. Like study." She
slapped the tortilla onto a sheet of waxed paper and reached
for more dough. "I wanted more of a life for you than I had.
In the grand scheme of things, tortilla-making is not that
important."

True, it wasn't. But there were times when I wished I could make them just the same. Wasn't the lack of that ability just another step in my estrangement from the ways of my people?

My mother must have caught the pensive look on my face, because she said gently, "There's some red pop in the icebox. Go get one for yourself." "Red pop" was what we had called cherry soda as kids; its presence in my mother's refrigerator even now was a comforting reminder of a time when everything had been simpler.

"Of course it's cranberry juice," Mama added.

I smiled and went to fetch myself one. "Because of the old health nut."

"That's right." Another tortilla slapped onto the waxed paper. "So what have you found out about Ciro?"

I pulled up a stool and said, "Well, for one thing, I found out Ciro left everything to you in his will."

Mama's hands slowed for a few seconds, then went on patting the tortilla dough. "That's not exactly true. As I already explained to Lieutenant Kirk, I don't really benefit much."

"Mama, how can you say that? His books sell very well. The literary rights—"

"Obviously, whoever told you about the will didn't know everything. I am Ciro's executor, yes, but the bulk of the money goes to the university, for a scholarship to be set up in his name. He asked me to oversee his literary rights because he trusted my judgment. And in return for that, he left me his personal possessions. It will probably be more trouble than it's worth to dispose of them."

"Oh."

"Who told you about the will?"

"Does it matter?"

She fixed me with a stern look. "Answer me."

"Mary Jaramillo. She said she witnessed it."

"That woman is nosy, and she has a big mouth and a small brain."

I couldn't contradict her there. Feeling relieved that the matter of the inheritance had been explained, I summarized what I'd found out about Ciro's murder since I'd seen her last.

When I was done, Mama stood frowning, rolling a ball of dough absently between her palms. "Maybe," she finally said, "this story of the slain soldiers has something to do with Ciro's trip to Bakersfield."

"Bakersfield? Why did he go there?"

"He hadn't yet, but he planned to. Next week."

"Why?"

"There were some documents at the historical society he wanted to look at."

"Documents about what?"

"He didn't say. And I didn't ask; I liked reading Ciro's finished manuscripts, but frankly, most of his research struck me as boring. I let him go on about it, but a lot of the time I never really listened."

I thought for a moment, sipping cranberry juice. "Did anyone else besides you know that Ciro was planning to go there?"

"It was no secret. Around the park, we're always careful to alert people when we're going to be away. It reduces the chances of burglary."

"Then his neighbors would have been sure to know," I said, thinking of Joe Garcia

"Of course."

Then I thought of Bakersfield and wrinkled my nose.

Mama glanced at me, concerned. "What is it, Elena?"

"It's awfully hot in Bakersfield at this time of year. I'm not going to like it there one bit."

Twelve

ON THE WAY back to the museum, I puzzled over the matter of Ciro's will—or, more specifically, the matter of what Mary Jaramillo had said about it. She claimed to have witnessed it, and a nosy woman like her would have been sure to thoroughly read any document to which she had been asked to affix her signature. But when she had talked to me, she'd mentioned nothing about the scholarship fund. All she had said in reference to my mother was "She gets everything."

Why? I wondered. Jealousy? A malicious desire to start a rumor? Or was it a deliberate ploy to cast suspicion on someone other than herself? If so, it was badly misdirected. I was more likely to believe my own mother than her, and the will could be produced at any moment for verification of its contents. It made no sense. No sense at all.

But then, people's actions didn't make sense a great deal of the time.

When I arrived at the museum, I was gratified to see that everything was running smoothly. Visitors were still coming in droves, and the donation box was stuffed with bills. Susana was at her desk, typing industriously, and she even favored me with a smile as she handed me my messages. There was nothing of importance in the stack, and I took care of them quickly before I called Dave Kirk again. I read off the two lists I'd gotten from Adela to him, then told him about Joe Garcia moving out of the park. He took down both the forwarding address Garcia had left and the license number of the U-Haul trailer. Encouraged, I went on to explain about the legend of the slain soldiers and Ciro's planned trip to the Bakersfield Historical Society.

To all of that, Kirk replied, "Huh."

"What do you mean, 'Huh'?"

"It's interesting, but I don't see what it has to do with the investigation. Ciro Sisneros must have made research trips all the time."

"The whole story of the slain soldiers started near Bakersfield. Ciro was probably going there to research some aspect of it."

"Huh."

"Dave—"

"I'm sorry, Elena, but it's not that much of a lead. Not enough to justify sending a man over there."

"What about sending me?"

"You?"

"I can take the time off from work." I shouldn't, really. There was a great deal to be done here—the new catalog, meetings with the volunteer who handled our publicity, studying the workload to see if I could manufacture a position for Emily Hitchens, appraising Abuela Felicia's paintings, to say nothing of policing Susana so she didn't close the place down and get everyone working on that damned float.

"Well. . . ." He paused. "You never know what you might turn up."

Mentally, I began reassigning tasks. Linda Trujillo was well qualified to oversee production on the catalog on her own. The meeting with the publicity woman could be shifted to next week. Emily and Abuela Felicia wouldn't starve if I took care of their problems a few days later than I'd planned. And as far as Susana—if she so much as touched that float before Saturday, I'd fire her.

"I'll go," I said.

"You'll be there in an unofficial capacity."

"I know."

"That means the department won't even pay for your gas."

"That's okay."

"Or lodging."

"Don't worry!"

"When are you leaving?"

"Tonight after work."

"Good. If you run into trouble or find out anything important, call me anytime." He gave me his home telephone number and hung up.

I looked at my watch. It was almost three. If I worked very hard, I could at least get one of my tasks done before leaving. I'd go to the basement right away and try to appraise those paintings.

I descended into the gloom of the basement, flicked on the fluorescent lights, and stood feeling the peace that always settled on me in that cool, quiet room. Around me ranged the glass-fronted shelves where artifacts were kept and the specially constructed racks that held paintings. The basement was orderly and serene, and I did some of my best thinking here. I checked the temperature-and-humidity gauge—the first of several such gauges I intended to install throughout the museum as the budget permitted and then went to work unwrapping the paintings. The first step would be to make a list of them; then I would study them more closely and assign a value to each.

As I worked, I noticed that although they were uniform in size, the paintings were done in two distinct styles. The older ones—signed with the initials *F. M.* for Felicia Martinez, Jesse's grandmother—showed better technique, and though the subject matter was grim, they had a certain charm that comes from historical distance. The modern paintings—unsigned—had been executed by a less competent artist, but that lack of skill was more than made up for by a raw emotion revealed in every brushstroke.

I held up one painting that depicted a group of men in confrontation in an orchard. I could feel the violence, barely restrained, as if the static figures were about to erupt into motion. It was as if I were looking at only one frame of a color newsclip of the events preceding a riot. Whoever had painted these scenes had been angry, very angry indeed. They disturbed me, made me shiver in the cool of the basement; and while my curator's instinct told me these paintings were very good, I knew I could not bear to have one in my home.

I continued listing the paintings by subject matter and artist—*F. M.* or *Unknown*. When I finished, I had itemized twenty-nine, only six by Abuela Felicia.

Twenty-nine? We'd counted them last night, and there had been thirty. Or was that right? It had been late, and I'd been tired; maybe I'd miscounted. I'd go upstairs and ask Emily if she remembered.

I went up to the little gift shop off the entry. Mrs. Ramirez, the older lady who couldn't add too well, was manning the cash register.

"Where's Emily?" I asked.

She blinked at my abrupt question. "Why, dear, she went home. At least two hours ago."

"Oh." I thought of Emily's fainting spell the night before. "Was she ill?"

"No, she seemed quite cheerful, in fact. Excited, as if she might have an important date or a party to go to. But didn't you talk with her?"

"No, I haven't seen her all day."

"That's odd." Mrs. Ramirez pursed her lips thoughtfully.

"Why is it odd?"

"Well, when I arrived, she asked me to begin watching the shop early. I didn't mind, even though I feel we volunteers should be responsible for the full time we sign up for—"

"Where did she go when she left you in charge?"

Mrs. Ramirez looked irritated at the interruption but said, "To the basement, looking for you."

"But I wasn't even in the building two hours ago."

"Well, whatever her reason, she thought you were in the basement. She went down there and came up a few minutes later with a parcel. I thought you had given it to her."

"How big a parcel?"

"About like this." She gestured off an area roughly the size of one of the labor-movement paintings.

So that was why there were only twenty-nine now. Emily had taken the thirtieth. But why? They weren't valuable. She couldn't sell it. . . . And then I thought of her fainting fit again. Had the cause of it, rather than hunger, been something in one of those paintings?

"Mrs. Ramirez," I said, "did she say where she was going?"

"Home, I think."

"Thank you."

I hurried through the courtyard to the office wing, once again told Susana she was in charge, got my purse, and left to find Emily.

The place where I'd dropped Emily off last night was in the area of the city called the Riviera. It was an attractive neighborhood, with houses terraced into the hills. The streets were curved in switchbacks, so one's neighbors several doors away were also one's neighbors up the hill. The house where Emily rented her "in-law" apartment—the extra suite that was supposed to be for family members only, and thus violated zoning laws in this area—had a garage directly on the street and a series of stone steps leading up to a wide lawn and then to the house. I climbed them, panting a little from the exertion, crossed a wide terrace with a panoramic view of the town and the sea, and rang the bell.

The old woman who answered was as tiny and stooped as

Abuela Felicia. Her white hair was done up in neat curls, and she leaned on an aluminum walker. When I asked for Emily, the web of fine wrinkles around her eyes deepened.

"They've gone away," she said.

"Gone away? Where?"

"I don't know. She came home about two hours ago and borrowed my car. I didn't mind letting her have it; I never drive, haven't for at least five years now."

"But she didn't say where she was going?"

"No. Is something wrong? Is Emily in some sort of trouble?"

She seemed so anxious that I hastened to reassure her. "No, there's no trouble. I'm Elena Oliverez, from the museum where she does volunteer work. Emily . . . has one of our paintings, and I wanted to get it back from her."

The woman looked thoughtful for a moment. "I guess I could give you the key to her apartment. She wouldn't mind." She moved away, carefully positioning the walker before each two steps, and returned in a while with the key. "It's around the left-hand side of the house. It's really the maid's quarters, but I haven't had a live-in maid in years. No one wants to live in anymore."

I took the key and crossed the lawn, wondering at the landlady's trusting nature. The door to the maid's quarters was set in a little vine-covered archway. I fitted the key into the lock and opened the door. The room was dark, with only small high windows, and I fumbled around on the wall until I found a light switch. The central bulb, shaded with a cheap white paper lantern, came on, revealing a single room with a tiny refrigerator and a hotplate on top of it. The open hide-a-bed took up most of the floorspace, and off to one side in a little alcove was a crib.

I went over there and picked up one of the stuffed toys, a red elephant with white polka dots and black velveteen ears. So the "they" the landlady had referred to were Emily and her baby—not Emily and the cat she'd claimed to have. Why had she hidden the child's existence from me? There was nothing wrong with having a baby, even if she was a single mother. Did I seem like such an ogre that I wouldn't understand?

Turning, I surveyed the rest of the room, but there was no sign of the painting. There wasn't much here, except for a small dresser and a shelf above the refrigerator that held one plate, one cup, one glass, and a couple of baby bottles. A saucepan stood on the burner, and some utensils sat next to the hotplate, but otherwise there was no cooking equipment. A couple of books—paperback mysteries—lay on a table next to the hide-a-bed, but there was no television, radio, or stereo. I wondered how Emily passed her time in this dreary little room, what she thought, whether she resented the poverty of her life. Finally I set the elephant back in the crib, locked the room, and went back to the main entrance of the house.

The little old lady still stood there, leaning on her walker. "Did you find what you were looking for?" she asked, glancing at my empty hands.

"No." I gave the key back to her. "She must have taken it with her. Did you notice if she had a large parcel when she left?"

The woman nodded. "Yes, she did. She treated it very carefully, made a special trip up from the garage for it. Then she left, with Tommy all bundled up in the basket she has for him."

"How did she seem? I mean, was she in good spirits? Happy?"

"I'd say she was more excited than happy. Nervous. She almost dropped the car keys when I gave them to her."

"And she didn't say when she'd be back?"

"All she said was 'soon.' I don't know what that means." The woman cocked her white head like a worried little bird.

"Emily *is* in some kind of trouble, isn't she? Did she steal that painting you mentioned?"

I didn't answer.

"And she's not coming back, is she?"

"I don't know."

"Oh dear." She looked as if she might start to cry. "I do hope she comes back. It's not the car—I don't mind about that; it's not doing me any good sitting down there in the garage. But I'll miss her. She's only been here a month, but I've come to rely on her so."

"She mentioned she runs errands for you."

"Oh my, yes. She buys the groceries and brings up the mail and the papers. Sometimes at night when I'm feeling badly she comes and sits with me. I taught her to play cards—gin rummy. It's been so nice, so *unlonely* since she's been here."

"What about the baby—Tommy? Doesn't he bother you, crying like babies do?"

"Tommy's a very good baby. I watch him while she's at work, you know. I didn't approve, her leaving him all alone down there, but Emily explained she couldn't afford anyone to come in and care for him. So I offered to help."

"How old is Tommy?"

"Oh, only about six months. He's a very *good* baby. I've enjoyed having him in the house. It reminds me of when mine were that age; those were happier times. I don't even mind that Tommy is part Mex." She paused then, studying my face. "Oh dear. You're Mexican. I've said the wrong thing, and I'm terribly sorry."

I was too busy taking in this last detail to be seriously offended. Besides, she was a product of a different time, when people thought it all right to refer to us as Mexes. The ones of her generation who used that term actually liked my people; if they didn't, they called us Spics.

"That's all right," I said gently.

She looked somewhat relieved, but her eyes were still troubled. "Do you think Emily and Tommy will come back?"

"I'm going to try to find them. I'll tell her you need her."

"I really do; I've come to rely on her so. Why, I don't even know how I'm going to get down to the street to fetch my evening paper. I always managed before, but even after only a month, that seems so long ago."

"Don't worry," I said. "I'll get your paper. And I'll try to send Emily back."

It was strange, I thought. She had said something offensive to me and I was trying to make up for her discomfort. But maybe what I was really trying to make up for was the fact that times had changed and left her behind—and all alone.

Thirteen

I HAD A fairly strong hunch where Emily had gone—to Ojai—and for a few minutes I considered trying to confirm it. But then I decided that the trip to the historical society in Bakersfield was more pressing. Once that was accomplished, I could deal with Emily on the way back. I went home, packed a bag with enough things for an overnight stay, and drove south to pick up Route 126 at Ventura.

At first the road was freeway, but then it narrowed to a two-lane highway that passed through orange groves whose trees hung heavy with fruit. Eventually it connected with Interstate 5, and I began the long descent over Tejon Pass into the San Joaquin Valley. At the Bakersfield cutoff, I turned northeast, and soon I was passing old, rundown housing tracts and trailer parks on the outskirts of town. The land was flat, stretching for miles toward the hills that were greatly diminished by the distance. I took what seemed to be a main downtown exit and drove through the heat-hazed streets looking for a place to stay.

I found it, lured by a huge sign on top of the Rancho Bakersfield Motel that read *Let's Eat!* The motel itself was a sprawling structure with a bleached-out turquoise roof that faintly resembled oxidized copper and many wings whose doors were painted alternately blue and red. When I saw another sign advertising a happy hour and dance contests, I nearly drove right past the entrance to the parking lot, but then I shrugged and pulled in near the office. The motel was convenient, didn't look overly expensive, and I was hungry enough to agree heartily with the sentiment expressed by the big sign. The clerk gave me a room in the nine-hundred wing—as far as possible, he assured me, from the bar where the dance contests were held.

"But you might enjoy the music," he added, handing me my copy of the credit-card slip. "Bakersfield *is* the country-and-western capital of California, you know."

I hadn't known, and all that information did was make me wonder what on earth I was doing here.

Once in the room—which had a blue door and was surprisingly comfortable—I checked the phone book and got the address for the historical society. It was on H Street. Then I went back to the office, looked at the map posted there, and found out that the street was only a few blocks from the motel. After a burger and fries in the coffee shop, I returned to my room to brood.

Why had I rushed over here tonight? I wondered. It certainly had been an ill-advised move. I could have stayed home in my own house, puttering and reading all evening, and driven to Bakersfield early in the morning. Instead, here I was, stuck in a motel in the country-and-western capital of California with only the spy novel I'd tossed into my bag at the last minute. The novel had been another bad idea; I didn't really like spy novels, and I certainly wasn't in the mood for one tonight. And there wasn't anything I wanted to watch on TV, not even the dreadful prime-time soap operas to which I am secretly addicted.

I wished now that I'd gone to Ojai before coming here. If Abuela Felicia had had a phone, I could have called her to ask if Emily had indeed appeared, wanting to know about the painting she had taken. I would sleep better knowing no harm had come to it. But at least for tonight, there was no way to find out.

I wandered around the room, feeling grouchier and grouchier, trying not to think about Emily and the painting. Finally, I got into bed and forced myself to begin the novel, stopping occasionally to listen to the country music that, despite the clerk's assurances to the contrary, came through loud and clear from the cocktail lounge. When I finally drifted off to sleep, my dreams were filled with sad songs about infidelity and love gone wrong.

I awoke the next morning still faintly depressed, ate a hurried breakfast of eggs and sausage, and was at the historical society when its doors opened at nine. It was housed in an old brick building downtown near the Fox Theater. The theater looked like a Moorish castle, and the historical society looked like a medieval fortress; together, they presented a strange combination in this agricultural town where trailers and old tract homes seemed to be the architectural staples.

The woman in charge of the historical society was short and dumpy. She had a cloud of light brown hair, thick blue-rimmed glasses, and a nice smile that revealed the most perfect set of teeth I'd ever seen. When I mentioned Professor Ciro Sisneros, her smile grew even wider.

"Of course. We were expecting him to visit this week, but so far he hasn't appeared."

I paused, uncertain whether to bring up the subject of Ciro's death. "Did Professor Sisneros have an appointment, then?"

"No, but he had made an inquiry." Now it was her turn to pause, suspicion coming into her eyes. "May I ask what your interest in the professor is?"

"Professor Sisneros is dead." I watched as dismay took the place of suspicion. "My mother, Gabriela Oliverez, is executor of his estate. I'm trying to locate some information he was planning to use in his new book; someone will have to finish it."

"Of course." The woman nodded absently, then reached into the side drawer of her desk and came up with a file. She pulled a clipping and two letters from it and pushed them across the desk to me. "The ad is how we first made contact with the professor, although naturally I knew him by reputation."

The clipping was from the classified advertising section of a state historical journal—the same one I'd seen on the shelves in Mary Jaramillo's living room. It read: *Anyone having information on the Legend of the Slain Soldiers or the Raoul Garcia family, please contact . . .* and was signed with Ciro's name and address. The first letter, from the historical society to Ciro, offered to let him look at three cartons of Garcia family documents in the society's possession. A letter from Ciro thanked them and said he would arrive in Bakersfield sometime this week.

I looked up at the woman. "Who were the Garcias?"

"Raoul Garcia was a labor leader from one of the national organizations in Washington, D.C. He came to Bakersfield in nineteen thirty-five to act as adviser to the local leaders. Later on, he settled in the area, near Weed Patch, I believe."

"Is he still living?"

"No. We received the documents as a bequest from his estate."

"I see. Is it possible for me to look at them?"

"Certainly. The resources of the society are available to anyone who asks, and we certainly want to aid you in completing Professor Sisneros's work."

So I spent the day—breaking only for a quick lunch—cooped up in a stuffy little room with the three cartons of old letters, diaries, and record books. At five o'clock, a clerk came in and told me the society was closing. Did I plan to come back the next day? she asked. If not, they would box up the materials and store them away again.

No, I said, I'd found what I'd come for. Although I hadn't finished with all the contents of the boxes, I'd been able to piece together what I thought was the real story of the slain soldiers.

Coming out into the late-afternoon heat, I crossed the street to where I'd parked my car, then stopped, staring at the left rear tire, which had gone completely flat. With a disgusted noise, I hurried around to the rear of the car, opened the hatchback, and looked for the spare. Only it wasn't there.

"*Maldito*," I said, clapping my hand to my forehead. I knew exactly where the spare was—in my garage, where I'd left it a couple of weeks ago. It was a regular tire, not the little collapsible one that had come with the car, and it took up a good deal of space. I'd had to load a large number of cartons containing artifacts we'd gotten on loan from a local collector, and thus had decided to make room by leaving the spare at home. Of course, I'd forgotten to put it back in the car.

Now what? Call Triple A. They'd know what to do. I looked around, spied a phone booth a block away, and hurried down there—past an inordinately large number of buildings housing fraternal organizations, including one from which two men in fezzes were emerging. I got the number for AAA, called and explained my problem, and then went to look for my card. Like the spare tire, it wasn't there. I'd renewed my membership late this year, and the card had come, but I'd neglected to sign it and put it in my wallet. And naturally I didn't remember my membership number.

They were sorry, the Triple A road service informed me, but under the circumstances there was nothing they could do to help.

I slammed down the receiver, more angry at myself than at them. Why didn't I take care of myself properly? I was always late paying bills, always neglectful of important personal details. Why? I liked to blame it on my time-consuming job, but underneath I knew that wasn't it. I just didn't *like* paying bills, just wasn't good with details.

I snatched up the telephone directory that hung on a chain

below the phone, and turned to *Tires* in the Yellow Pages. There was a whole column of dealers, but when I began calling I quickly realized that few would be open after five in the afternoon. The one who finally answered his phone would only come out and deliver the tire if I gave him my Visa card number. I did, and went back to the car to wait.

An hour passed. No tire dealer. I occupied my time by thinking about the Raoul Garcia family and the slain labor leader, Alberto Ortega. Finally I went back to the phone and called the tire dealer. The person who answered informed me they had had other emergency calls. I was to sit tight and they'd get to me eventually.

I sat tight. The downtown area became deserted, devoid even of fraternal-order members in fezzes. The sun began to sink, but the temperature didn't fall with it.

I thought of Ciro, his ad in the state historical journal. I had a hunch that this was where his killer had found out about his interest in the legend of the slain soldiers. Who would read a historical journal? Mary Jaramillo. Mary, who subscribed to the one in which Ciro had advertised. Mary, who was about the right age to have a vested interest in someone stirring up that legend. But the family involved had been called Garcia. A common name, that was true, but was it too much of a coincidence that one of the suspects in this case was also called Garcia? And then there was another suspect—or, more precisely, the wife of one—Gloria Walters. What if her maiden name had been Garcia? She was the right age, too—in her seventies.

After another hour, I was about to go back to the phone booth, but as I reached for the door handle, a truck with *Stan's Tire Service* painted on the side roared up. A kid of about eighteen jumped down, took one look at my car, and said, "Uh-oh."

I got out, stretching my cramped limbs, and said, "What do you mean, 'uh-oh'?"

"They gave me the wrong-size tire."

I went limp against the side of the car. "You've got to be joking."

"Nope. Tire I've got won't fit no way."

I looked at my watch. It was well after seven, and I wanted to get back to Santa Barbara and talk with Dave Kirk tonight. "How long will it take you to get the right size?"

He looked at his watch too. "I'm already on overtime, lady."

I gritted my teeth and squeezed my eyes shut, trying not to scream. Apparently the boy thought I was going to cry instead, because he said, "Don't take it so hard, lady. I'll get you your tire. I can use the bread anyway." And then he got back in the truck and zoomed off.

I sat in the car, this time thinking of nothing more than how long it would take me to get back to Santa Barbara. In my imagination, the journey over the pass seemed endless; the distance through the orange groves to the coast and then north to home stretched out to infinity. And, on top of that, I was hungry. Starving, in fact.

The boy returned with the tire in fifteen minutes, put it on quickly, and accepted a five-dollar tip I really couldn't afford. I started the car, drove back to the Rancho Bakersfield Motel, and had a quick burger in the coffee shop, listening to the country musicians warming up for another dance contest. Fortified, I drove the VW to the nearest freeway entrance and turned south toward Interstate 5.

It wasn't until much later, on the long ascent toward the summit of Tejon Pass, that I noticed a pair of headlights holding at a steady distance behind me. Some cars would speed past, others would drop back and eventually disappear; but this pair of lights stayed about nine or ten car lengths back, even though my speed varied on the steep grade. When I changed lanes a few times, the other car did too.

I told myself that it didn't have to mean anything. It could simply be coincidence. Or the driver of the other car might be nervous on the mountainous road; perhaps he felt safer following the beacon of someone else's taillights.

Still, I kept glancing in my rearview mirror. I speeded up and changed lanes again. The headlights followed.

All right, I thought, so what if someone *is* following you? What harm can he do here on the freeway? You're in your own car with the doors locked. You've got plenty of gas and a brand-new tire. Let him follow you all the way to Santa Barbara if he wants.

But I began to feel edgy, and my fingers gripped the wheel harder.

It was half past ten by the time I reached the turnoff for Route 126, south of Castaic. The headlights still appeared in my rearview mirror as I exited from the interstate. Once I was on the two-lane road, I pressed down on the accelerator and watched the speedometer needle edge up over seventy. The distance between my car and the headlights remained constant. I slowed down to sixty. In spite of the decrease, the other car came no closer.

I was really edgy now but still felt no immediate threat. After all, I couldn't be hurt by someone who was merely following me. I continued along the road, occasionally glancing in the mirror. Traffic was light in both directions, and on either side the orange groves spread dark and quiet. A three-quarter moon hung high in the west.

I had just begun to relax a little when a sharp curve appeared ahead. I had to brake quickly, and apparently the driver of the other car didn't react as fast, because he came right up behind me, almost on my bumper. I held my Rabbit to the curve, then put on speed. This time the other car didn't drop back.

I pressed the accelerator to the floor. The lights followed, dangerously close. Panicked, I edged over toward the shoulder, hoping he would pass me. Instead he pulled over too and nudged my bumper.

"*Por Dios,* what is he doing?" I said aloud. Gripping the steering wheel, my palms sweating, I urged the car over eighty. The lights glared in my mirror, then began to pull around me.

I glanced over. All I could see was the car's long dark hood. It was only inches away from the side of my car, forcing me farther and farther onto the shoulder. Fear made me curse and lean on my horn, but the car didn't pull away. Another curve loomed up ahead, its white guardrail leaping out in the combined glare of our headlights.

I braked frantically, my heart racing. My car skidded and slammed into the one beside me. The impact tore the wheel from my hands and I hurled myself sideways on the seat as the car hit the guardrail. Metal screamed against metal, and then I felt the VW leave the ground and fly sideways. With a wrenching crash, it hit the ground on the passenger's side, jarring but not really hurting me. I hung suspended by my seatbelt, the gearshift knob pressing into my ribs.

The sudden silence, broken only by my gasping, sobbing breath, was almost as shocking as the crash. I managed to grab the seatbelt and then pull myself up so I could unhook it. It released and I dropped down against the passenger door, where I huddled, shaking all over and listening for footsteps. Everything was silent.

Where was the car that had forced me off the road? Had it merely driven off, or was my assailant lurking somewhere outside? If he was there and I tried to crawl out of the car—

And then I smelled gas. Like Ciro's trailer a few nights before, the car might explode. I pulled myself into a crouch, reached up, and pushed the driver's-side door open. There was no sound outside. I stood up and peered out into the surrounding darkness. I saw no one.

I hoisted myself through the door, dropped to the ground, and looked around. The car was resting on its side against a utility pole. Straight ahead was the high embankment that led up to the road, and on it a car idled, its headlights bright on the torn guardrail; a dark figure was just getting out of it. I quickly turned and ran the other way, toward the railroad tracks and orange grove beyond.

Then I tripped on one of the rails, and my right sandal twisted and came off. Stopping, I wrenched the left one free and kept going. I ran deep into the grove, stumbling among windfall oranges and knocking over a ladder that was propped against one of the trees. Finally I grasped a tree trunk, leaning against it and panting. No one had followed me. I could hear nothing but the distant sound of a truck shifting gears on the highway.

Who was the person who had run me off the road? Was he some lunatic who got his kicks trying to kill people on dark highways? Given the state of the world today, I could believe it.

But I could also believe it might have been someone with a more definite purpose. Someone who knew why I'd gone to Bakersfield, had followed me there, had known what I'd find out. And had wanted to stop me from returning to Santa Barbara with that information. If that was the reason I'd been forced off the road, there was no way I would return to my car now. It wasn't drivable anyway.

I leaned against the tree, calmer now, trying to formulate a plan of action. The best thing to do, I decided, was to get out of this grove and contact the Highway Patrol. And the safest way out of here would be through the trees until I was far from the scene of the wreck. From what I remembered of the drive over to Bakersfield, these groves stretched for miles and the spur tracks paralleled the road. If I moved along in the shelter of the trees, keeping the rails in sight, I wouldn't become disoriented and wander too far from the highway. Once I was far enough away from here, I could climb the embankment and flag down a car.

I went back to the very edge of the grove, located the tracks, and started walking west. It was quiet out here, with only the occasional sound of traffic or a nocturnal birdcall. The citrus smell was pleasant, reminiscent of home and my sunny breakfast nook, and it helped to calm me. I walked for at least half an hour, ducking back under the trees if a car's headlights swept over the grove when the road curved. Finally, I decided I had come far enough and climbed the embankment. It was steep, and I fell to my knees twice, but I finally gained the road's shoulder.

The rest was fairly easy. The first four cars I tried to flag down passed me by, but the fifth—an old van driven by a fat, aging hippie—picked me up and took me straight to the Highway Patrol station in Santa Paula. After reporting the accident, I asked to use the telephone, called Santa Barbara, and asked Dave Kirk to come get me.

Fourteen

I PRESSED THE button on the coffee grinder and watched the beans whirl and disintegrate into fine powder. Then I upended the grinder, dumped coffee into the filter, and poured water into the top of the brewer. While it dripped, I leaned wearily against my kitchen counter.

I could hear Dave Kirk pacing around in the living room. I should probably go out there and begin my long, involved explanations of what I'd found out, but I didn't feel up to it. I was bruised, battered, and my emotions were out of kilter. I needed more time to sort things out.

When Kirk had arrived at the Santa Paula Highway Patrol station, I'd been dozing in my chair. My first awareness of his presence had come when he'd put his hands on my shoulders and knelt down to get a look at my face.

"Are you all right?" he said.

I opened my eyes and met his. And in them—previously so bland and unreadable—was confirmation of what I'd only suspected until now. His expression went beyond mere concern; there was warmth there, affection, and a touch of anxiety that I might not be in as good shape as I'd claimed over the phone.

"I'm fine now," I said.

And then Dave—that strange, imperturbable Anglo—had put his arms around me and cradled me against him, one hand coming up to smooth my curls. "Thank God," he said softly.

He held me for a long moment, then released me and led me outside to his car.

On the drive to Santa Barbara, we'd discussed how I'd been run off the road, then lapsed into a stilted silence, unable to speak, because our relationship had moved onto a new plane, one where neither of us seemed to feel at ease. And when we'd arrived at my house, Dave had received my offer of coffee and a fuller explanation of my findings, solemnly as if coming into my house was some sort of irrevocable step. I sensed he was as surprised by his feelings as I was, and also shared the same reservations about a deeper relationship. When I'd left him to make the coffee, he'd been looking around my living room—even though he'd been there before—as if he'd just walked out of the airport in some exotic foreign land.

Well, in a way wasn't my world exotic and foreign to him? Just as his was to me? I supposed that had always been part of the attraction Anglos held for me; they thought and lived differently than I did. Becoming involved with one was, in a sense, a ticket out of the life I'd known and into an exciting new realm.

But that was before. Lately I'd noticed a settling in me, a desire to come to terms with my heritage. And coming to terms meant sticking with the people and customs I knew best. Leave it to Dave Kirk to decide to care about me *now*, after that settling process had begun. How was I to reconcile the strong attraction I felt for him with my new attitude?

The coffee was finished. I poured two cups and carried them to the living room. In the doorway, I stopped, stifling a giggle when I saw what Dave was doing.

He was standing in front of my colonial-period chest, looking at a pottery sun face that I kept there. The piece was by an artist named Candelario, and it was one of my favorites—a bright yellow sun with a hooked nose; intensely focused eyes; and a red mouth framing jagged, gapped teeth. Sun ray in different colors protruded all around it. Dave had extended his index finger toward the mouth, and as I watched he stuck it in there, between the teeth, looking both fascinated and a little timid.

"It doesn't bite," I said.

He pulled his finger back and turned toward me, looking embarrassed at being caught at child's play. Then he grinned. "Sure looks like it could."

I set the coffee down and motioned for him to sit on the couch. Then I pulled up my rocker and sat down too. He sipped coffee, nodding appreciatively, and gestured at the sun face. "What's it supposed to be?"

"The sun, of course."

"I know that. But why?"

"What do you mean, why?"

"Why does it exist at all? It's weird."

"Well, yes. It's surrealistic. But the nice thing is that the artist doesn't know he's being surrealistic. He's just having fun; that's what makes it so enjoyable."

Dave glanced dubiously at it. "Maybe."

If this relationship went any further, I realized Dave Kirk was going to receive quite an education in what he would refer to as "weird art." I smiled, thinking of how he would react to some of the pieces we had at the museum, pieces that made Candelario's work look tame.

"What's so funny?" he asked.

"You."

"You want to explain that?"

"Not now."

"Soon, then."

"Soon. Right now I have other explaining to do."

"About what you found out in Bakersfield."

"Yes." I told him about Ciro's ad in the state historical journal and his interest in the Garcia family.

"Garcia," he said. "Could they be any relation to Joe?"

"I wondered about that myself. There wasn't any mention of him in the documents I read, and it's a fairly common name, but all the same there may be a connection."

"So the documents you looked at belonged to this family."

"Yes. Primarily to Raoul Garcia, a labor organizer, and his daughter, Beatriz. There were three cartons of them ranging from union records, ledgers, and correspondence to personal letters and a diary. It was the personal things that told me what Ciro had been interested in."

"And what was that?"

"The legend of the slain soldiers—the story that Jesse Herrera's grandmother told me the other night."

"I remember. Go on."

"In the legend, the leader of the slain men, Alberto Ortega, has always been portrayed as a selfless man, devoted to his people and the laborers' cause. He had led a somewhat dissolute life where it came to women, but at the time of his death he had settled down and planned to marry the daughter of an Anglo landowner. People said their marriage would forge a new understanding between the growers and the *campesinos*."

"Who was the woman?"

"Victoria Piazza. Her father was a vintner, owned a lot of acreage in the hills near Ojai. While he was Italian, he had a great affinity for the Hispanic people, so he didn't object when Victoria fell in love with Alberto Ortega. An unusual attitude for the times."

"And so Ortega married her?"

"No. He was killed before the wedding could take place. Victoria apparently never got over his death and drowned herself a few years later, in the sea at Refugio Beach, where Ortega was murdered."

Dave sipped coffee and frowned. "Maybe I'm not following what you're telling me, but I don't understand why Ciro Sisneros's interest in this would have gotten him killed."

"I'm getting to that. I said there was a diary in the Garcia documents. It belonged to Beatriz, the daughter of the labor-union organizer." The diary had actually been a series of clothbound account ledgers in which the young woman had inscribed her experiences. Their pages had been covered with a bold, forward-slanting script that disregarded the columns and lines, as well as conventional spelling or grammar. And the story told in that dynamic and erratic hand had shattered once and for all the legend of the slain soldiers.

"From reading the diary, anyone could tell that Beatriz Garcia was a strong-willed woman," I went on. "Fiery-tempered and as active in the labor movement as either her father or Ortega. Raoul Garcia was a widower, and he'd taken his daughter everywhere with him; prior to coming to California, they'd been in Colorado, where they'd worked to organize the Spanish-American grape pickers. Beatriz was extremely free-thinking for a woman of those times, and she'd had a number of lovers. When they came to the San Joaquin Valley, she took up with Alberto Ortega."

"And he left her for the Piazza woman."

"Not exactly. According to the diary, Ortega originally wasn't in love with Victoria Piazza. What had attracted him was the land she stood to inherit."

"Meaning Ortega wasn't the selfless soul he's been portrayed as."

"Yes. And Beatriz Garcia didn't mind that aspect of his character—she was also accustomed to doing whatever she had to to get her way. She didn't view the relationship with Ortega as permanent or believe in the institution of marriage. So long as Ortega would remain her lover after the marriage took place, she would be happy."

"She said all this in the diary?"

"Yes. While I was reading it, I wondered how genuine her resistance to permanent ties was, since she seemed to be very much in love with Ortega. But she aborted his child when she became pregnant by him, rather than marry him. That means she was serious." The account of the abortion had been cold and matter-of-fact enough to shock me. Modern and liberal as I considered myself, I knew that if I were ever faced with such a decision, it would not be one I'd make as easily as Beatriz Garcia had.

"Anyway," I went on, "Beatriz's carefully controlled world began to get out of hand when Ortega fell in love with his fiancée. She suspected what was happening long before he admitted it either to himself or to her. Finally, she confronted him with it. He confessed to a growing affection for Victoria but promised not to leave Beatriz. For a time he wavered back and forth, reluctant to let go of either woman. But on the night before he was forced to flee to Refugio, he finally broke with Beatriz. The diary ended there. I found out the rest of it from a letter."

"From whom?"

"Beatriz to her father, Raoul Garcia." The letter had been written in the same bold hand as the diary, but it was more erratic, as if the author had been coming apart emotionally— as she undoubtedly had been. "Beatriz was enraged by Ortega's betrayal. She found out, from one of the men in the labor union, where he and his companions had gone. And she followed them there, to Refugio, for a final confrontation, in which she demanded he break off his engagement to Victoria. He refused, once again telling her it was over between them. Beatriz then shot him, and before his companions could restrain her, she shot them, too. The letter admitting all this was written some days later, mailed from Los Angeles. It's the last document in the Garcia papers that mentions her, so I assume she just disappeared."

"Why would her father save something so incriminating?"

I shrugged. "He probably meant to destroy it before his death, but he was disabled by a stroke and incapable of winding up his affairs. The documents, by direction of his will, went to the historical society and sat around in cartons for many years."

Dave looked thoughtful, then said, "I still don't quite see the connection between this and Ciro Sisneros."

"Ciro had some inkling that there was more to the story of the slain soldiers than everyone assumed. Maybe he'd talked with somebody who had heard a rumor, I don't know. But however he got onto it, once he suspected, there was no way he wasn't going to try to find out the truth. I knew Ciro; he could be awfully tenacious when it came to historical accuracy. His mistake was to let it be known that he was looking into it. And someone who didn't want the true story exposed stopped him."

"But why? It's an old murder. Who would care anymore?"

"Maybe Beatriz Garcia has descendants who don't want her exposed as a murderess. Family honor is part of the Hispanic culture. Many of our traditions are breaking down, but the Garcia clan may be old-fashioned."

"Or the woman may still be alive. She'd be in her seventies."

"I hadn't thought of that. If she is, there's no statute of limitations on murder. Another thing I thought of was the Hispanic labor movement. If the legend of the slain soldiers is exposed as the result of a cheap love triangle, and the hero of it as an unscrupulous man who would marry in order to get his hands on some land, the spirit of the movement could suffer at a time when it can ill afford to. The movement depends on a lot of intangibles like that legend. And if the movement weakens, there's money to be lost."

Dave nodded, his gaze wandering around the room and finally coming to rest on the sun face. I stretched and yawned.

He looked at me. "You must be exhausted."

"Yes, I am." Now that I'd told my story, a bone-deep weariness had set in.

"Try to get some sleep." He stood up.

I looked at my watch. It was after five in the morning; in

four more hours I was due at the office. I couldn't afford to take any more time off—and there was still the problem of Emily Hitchens and the missing painting.

"Sleep," Dave repeated. "We'll worry about these other things later." He leaned forward and kissed me on the forehead, then went to the door.

I stared after him, wondering if by "these other things" he meant Ciro Sisneros and the slain soldiers, or Elena Oliverez and Dave Kirk.

Fifteen

I AWOKE WITH a start at noon and panicked because I was late for work. Then I realized it was Saturday. While I often worked on Saturday, I rarely put in an appearance until afternoon, and then the day was devoted to housekeeping chores and cleaning up the details of the week. It didn't matter if I went in on time or not, particularly today, when I needed to attend to the matter of Emily Hitchens.

I dragged the extension phone into bed with me, called Susana, and told her I wouldn't be in until midafternoon. "And when I arrive, I want that float finished," I said. "I have to approve it before it can be driven in the parade."

"Why, Elena? Don't you think we will do a good enough job to suit you?" Her voice was cross, like a petulant child's.

"It's not that. But I *am* in charge and I should okay things like that."

"If you are in charge, why do you spend so little time here?"

Usually I wouldn't have stood for such impertinence from an employee, but she did have a point. "Because I have other duties as well," I said defensively. "Today's errand involves the purchase of Jesse's grandmother's paintings." And it did, in a way.

"Well . . . what time will you come to see the float?"

"Maybe around three."

"Maybe?"

"I can't be sure of the exact time."

"But, Elena, I must wash my hair and get ready for Fiesta—"

"Susana, on a normal Saturday you work until five anyway."

"But this is special!"

I sighed, thinking back to when I had been as young as Susana. I, too, had worried about my hair and what dress to wear. "All right, I'll try to get there as early as possible. And then everybody can go home."

"Thank you, Elena." Her voice held a note of quiet surprise.

I hung up the phone, shaking my head. Was I really as much of an *osa negra* as Susana's manner implied? I didn't know, and right at the moment I didn't have time to think about it.

Next I called Emily Hitchens's number, on the off chance she might have returned home. When there was no answer, I tried her landlady, whose name and number I had taken down before leaving there the other day. No, she told me, there had been no sign of Emily or the baby. And now she was worried about her car.

I told her I would try to find them and hung up again, thinking about cars myself. The Rabbit had been hauled to a wrecking yard by now, and I would have to deal with the insurance company on Monday, then see about replacing it. But right now I needed transportation. Nick had an old clunker that I'd borrowed on occasion when the VW had been in the shop. But asking Nick for the car meant explaining what had happened. And explaining to Nick meant explaining to my mother, who would fuss and carry on even though I hadn't been hurt. Well, I'd just have to face that ordeal, because I couldn't accomplish anything that I intended to today without a car.

I called Nick and explained the situation. As I'd expected he said I could have the car. But the price he extracted was that I come to the trailer park with him and reassure Mama that all was well.

"Couldn't we just not tell her?" I suggested.

"Me keep something from Gabriela? Hah! You know how she worms things out of you."

"Well, maybe just not tell her until Monday or so?"

"How am I going to explain where the Dodge is?"

"You're right; it's impossible. When can you come get me?"

"Is an hour okay? I've got some errands to run on the way."

An hour would make it nearly one-thirty. The explanations to my mother could either take a long or a short time, depending on her reaction to them—and on how well I explained. And I'd promised Susana I'd try to get to the museum early. Still, I was in no position to insist Nick drop everything and rush down here.

"An hour's fine."

Nick arrived two hours later in his old pink-and-gray Dodge with the swooping tailfins. Its backseat was loaded with grocery bags, paper plates and cups, rolls of crepe paper, and five piñatas. "Last-minute additions to the list," he said as I got in. "Blame your mother. She thinks a party will help people get over Ciro's death, so she's talked herself into a party mood."

"I hope I won't wreck it."

"Probably you'll only add to the lunacy." Nick looked disapproving; he liked a quiet, orderly existence, and this party had disturbed it.

Once at the park, I helped him take the fruits of his errands into the rec center. Adela Hernandez looked out of the office, her face becoming even harder than usual when she saw us, and then she slammed the door of her little sanctuary. Obviously Adela didn't approve of parties any more than Nick did. When we finished the unloading, we walked over to my mother's trailer where—much to my surprise—we found her having coffee with Mary Jaramillo. Mary was not a sociable, coffee-klatching type, and her presence there struck me as strange.

"Elena," Mama said, "why aren't you at work?"

I looked to Nick for help, but he had turned his back to me and was rummaging through the refrigerator. "I'm taking the day off. I have outside business to attend to."

"Museum business?"

"Yes." I looked at Mary. She was watching me intently, a disapproving expression on her face.

"As I told you, Gabriela," she said, "the girl spends more time away from her desk than at it."

I just glared at her, not responding to the barbed remark. In a moment, she flushed and looked away.

"If you're on museum business," Mama said, "what are you doing here?"

"I . . ." I looked at Nick again. He was pouring cranberry juice. "I needed to borrow Nick's car."

"Why? What's wrong with yours?"

"It's not working."

Nick cleared his throat.

"It's been wrecked," I added.

Mama's face grew into lines of concern. "Elena! Were you driving?"

"Of course I was driving. It's my car."

"Are you hurt?" She half-rose from the table.

"Do I look hurt?"

She peered at me. "Not that I can see. But you can't always tell. That time you had the concussion—"

But Mary saved us from a discussion of that incident. She pushed her muumuu-swathed girth from her chair and said, "Gabriela, the girl looks fine." Then she added to me, "Here, you take my chair and tell your mother all about it."

The note of rationality in her voice seemed to calm my mother. She sat back down and folded her arms, waiting.

"Mary," I said, "I don't mean to interrupt your visit."

"I was about to go anyway." She stepped aside and waved me toward the chair, then went to the door, telling Mama she'd see her at the party. Nick, the old coward, also chose that moment to escape.

"So," Mama said sternly, "how did you come to wreck a perfectly good nine-thousand-dollar car?"

I explained about the car and also about my research in Bakersfield. When I finished, she sat very still, worry creasing her usually smooth brow. "I am sorry I ever involved you in this," she finally said.

"Now don't go feeling guilty."

"I am, however. I had a feeling the night that trailer exploded. I had a feeling then that something bad would happen."

Mama's "feelings" were legendary—and not always accurate. "Well, it wasn't anything all that bad. I've never liked the Rabbit anyway. It was a poor choice, and now I'll have a chance to get something I'll be happier with."

"It's not the car, Elena. The thought of you, all alone in that orange grove, with some . . . some *loco* stalking you—"

"Mama, please."

She was silent, and I thought I saw a wet gleam in her eyes. Quickly I said, "Mama, did anybody besides you know I was going to Bakersfield?"

She glanced away from me. "Why do you ask?"

"Well, if this person who ran me off the road wasn't just some random crazy, it must have been someone who knew I was going there and why."

"Oh." She began smoothing out the tablecloth with her work-worn fingers.

"Mama, who did you tell?"

"Well . . . Nick, of course."

"Who else?"

"Well, I was out at the pool and I may have mentioned it to a few people."

"May have?"

"Did."

"Who?"

"Well, just the usual crowd at the pool."

"And who is that?"

"Oh, Mary. And the Walters. Like I said, Nick. A few others."

"Mama, don't you think that might have been a little fool hardy? This is a murder we're dealing with—"

She looked up, her eyes flashing. "All right, it was foolish I admit that. I am an old woman and sometimes I don't think before I speak. Can I help it that I am proud of my daughter Proud that she would try to help find out who killed my friend?"

She looked so defiant, yet so guilty that I felt sorry for her and quit scolding. "It's okay, Mama. Probably it didn't do any harm." I paused, then added, "By the way, what was Mary doing here before? She's not exactly the type to drop in for coffee, is she?"

"No, she's not. I wondered too when I heard her at the door."

"What did she talk about?"

"Ciro, mostly. I think she's gotten it into her head that she should be the one to finish his book."

"Did she say anything about me?"

"Only asked if I'd heard from you since you returned from Bakersfield."

I nodded. "Mama, does Mary have a car?"

"Yes, an old Buick."

"What color?"

"Gray . . . black. Some neutral color, anyway."

"What about the Walters?"

"Something similar. I don't pay much attention to cars, you

know." Mama had never even had a driver's license, and when she rode with Nick or me, she was extremely wary.

I frowned, thinking of the dark-colored car that had forced me off the road. It could have been an older American model, like a Buick.

"Elena," Mama said, "you don't think—"

"I don't think anything yet. And don't you go mentioning it around the pool, or anyplace else."

"I have learned my lesson."

"Good." I stood up.

"Now where are you going?"

"To the museum, to make sure the float isn't a total disaster."

"And then?"

"I have to see someone about a painting."

"You aren't going to involve yourself in this business about Ciro any further, are you? I have a feeling—"

"No, Mama," I lied. "I'll leave it to the police."

But from the look on her face, I knew she didn't believe me.

The float was nowhere near a disaster. In fact, it looked good, almost as good as the actual *camaleone* after which it had been patterned. Susana flushed with pleasure when I said so and bustled inside to bring everyone a celebratory beer. When we'd drunk our toasts, I sent everybody home and closed up early—feeling less like an *osa negra* than I had that morning. Then, in the quiet of my office, I made a last call to Emily Hitchens's landlady. Emily and the baby were still missing. I reassured the old woman as best as I could. Then I set the museum's alarm system, got into Nick's old Dodge, and started out for Ojai.

Sixteen

ALTHOUGH IT WAS after five o'clock when I finally got to Ojai, the little town was crowded with tourists. They ambled in and out of the shops and galleries, wandered across the street without regard for cars, and blocked traffic while waiting for parking spaces. I muttered and cursed, finding Nick's big old Dodge harder to handle than the Rabbit, and by the time I started out of town toward Abuela Felicia's house, I was in a thoroughly bad humor.

It had been sunny and clear in Santa Barbara, but here in the hills unseasonable dark clouds lowered over the landscape. They imparted a grim, grayish-purple cast to the vegetation and made the shadows of the underbrush ominous. I tried not to let my imagination run wild as I steered the clumsy old car up the narrow road toward the ranch.

When I got to the stone arches that led to the ranch's entrance, I pulled the car up under the low branches of a gnarled oak tree. I realized that this was a melodramatic and probably unnecessary maneuver, but the need to approach quietly and on foot seemed paramount to me. I went down the driveway, skirted the old ranch house, and was about to cross to Abuela Felicia's cottage when the old woman came out.

She started when she saw me, and turned to go back inside. Then she glanced down at the baby bottle in her hand and shrugged. The bottle was clear evidence to me that Emily and her son, Tommy, were here, and apparently Abuela Felicia had decided she couldn't hide the fact from me.

I went up to her and said in Spanish, "So Emily did come to you."

She nodded, her eyes—so strangely youthful, like her grandson's—searching my face, trying to gauge my feelings.

"She brought the painting," I said, "because she wanted to know who the artist was."

"Not who. Where."

"Ah, she already knew who, from the style."

"Yes."

"But why did she stay, once you told her?"

The old woman looked down at the baby bottle again.

"I see," I said. "She left Tommy with you. Emily seems to have made a habit of leaving him with others—first her landlady, now you." When Abuela Felicia didn't reply, I added, "Who is the artist she was looking for? The baby's father?"

Again she didn't reply, merely staring down at the white plastic bottle in her hand. I said, "May I see the baby?"

Quickly, she looked up, and then her eyes strayed toward the barn. I realized she had been coming out of the house with the bottle, not going in. But why on earth would she keep the baby in the barn? Surely his small presence wouldn't crowd her out of her cottage. Unless. . . .

I turned and started over there.

"Elena," the old woman called, "leave them alone. They have had a hard enough time."

I stopped. "A hard time? Maybe. Emily didn't confide in me. What she did was steal one of the paintings from the museum—that's stealing from you as well, you know. And he took her landlady's car and didn't return it. The woman is worried sick—more about Emily and the child than her automobile."

"She plans to return both the car and the painting."

"Then why doesn't she do so, rather than hide out in your barn? What kind of place is that for her and her child?"

Abuela Felicia looked at me for a long time, sorrow dulling her eyes. Finally she said, "Perhaps you had better talk with Emily." We crossed to the barn door, me slowing my steps to her halting ones.

They were at one end, in the wide space between the two rows of empty stalls, sleeping bags and old blankets spread on the floor. The light of a Coleman lantern elongated their shadows, casting them upward against the stone foundation and massive wood beams. The baby, a chubby infant of about six months, lay asleep in a crib improvised from blankets. Emily sat nearby, watching him, her face aglow in the lamp light. A few feet away, leaning against one of the stalls, sat a handsome young man with shaggy black hair and an untrimmed mustache—the baby's father. He had a sketchpad propped on one knee and his charcoal stick moved over it in quick, sure motions.

Emily and the man looked up when we came in, and panic showed in their faces. The man dropped the charcoal and sketchpad, then jumped to his feet. He bolted into one of the opposite stalls, and Emily ran after him. The baby stirred and began to cry.

"Wait, Tomas," Abuela Felicia called authoritatively. "I think it's all right."

I turned to the old woman. "So that's why she's still here. She found him."

She nodded, but her eyes were on the stall. There was muffled conversation within, and then Emily and the man called Tomas emerged. She held him protectively by the wrist, and he followed slowly, his expression wary, as if he had been in flight for a long time and could not quite believe this was not an occasion for further running.

The baby was crying louder now. Emily dropped Tomas' wrist and went to the child, cradling him to her until his wail stopped. Then she turned to me and said, "You've come about the painting." Her head was held high, her voice defiant— very unlike the self-effacing woman I'd previously known.

"That, and your landlady's car. She's worried about you."

"I'm sorry; I didn't mean for her to be." Emily looked genuinely regretful. "I'll return the car to her tomorrow. You can take the painting now, if you like. I've no further use for it."

"Because you've found the artist." I motioned at the man. "Aren't you going to introduce us?"

She hesitated. "Look, Elena, please just go away. Take the painting and forget you ever knew me. Forget what you've seen here."

"Why?"

"Because if you don't, you'll wreck the only chance the three of us have."

"Tomas is in trouble, isn't he? He's hiding from the police."

It was merely an educated guess, but Emily's defiance crumbled and she looked helplessly at him. His muscles tensed, and again he seemed to steel himself for flight. Then Abuela Felicia said in Spanish, "I think it is time you all talked."

Tomas's head jerked toward her.

"I do not know Elena well," the old woman added, "but I know of her. She has been a good friend to my grandson in his time of trouble. She is fair."

The young man looked appraisingly at me, then shrugged and went back to where he had been sitting. Dropping to the floor, he said in heavily accented English, "Then we will talk."

Emily relaxed visibly and sat down also, still cradling the baby. Abuela Felicia said, "I will go to the house and reheat the bottle; it has grown cold." She walked slowly from the barn, and I sat down at a point equidistant from Emily and Tomas.

I looked pointedly at him, and he said, "My name is Tomas Dominguez. Perhaps you have heard of me?"

It seemed I had, but I couldn't place where.

When I shook my head, he went on. "I was a laborer, in the orchards near Visalia. Worked with the union, organizing. Until three months ago."

Now I remembered when I'd heard of him—at the dinner party Carlos had taken me to, where the people had talked about the labor unrest. I waited.

"There was a foreman. A real *hijo de puta*. We'd had run-ins before. This time it was a bad one. I beat him pretty good. Later that night someone finished the job for me. Shot him. Local law had it in for me because of the organizing; they were going to arrest me. I ran."

The parallel to the slain soldier Alberto Ortega was obvious. No wonder Emily had been so touched by the story, tears gleaming in the firelight as Abuela Felicia had told it.

I said, "And you left your wife and child behind."

"I'm not Tomas's wife," Emily said softly. "Not yet. We were waiting until we could afford to get married. I was still living at home with my family."

"How did they feel about your having the baby?"

"They weren't too happy, but they're good people, and they stood behind me."

"Then why did you leave there?"

"I had to find Tomas. It had been three months with no word from him. I was afraid something terrible had happened. A mutual friend told me he might be near Santa Barbara. He said there was a woman down here—he didn't know who or exactly where—who had been active in the labor movement in the thirties. She had a big, lonely place in the country and often had been known to help people in trouble."

"Abuela Felicia."

"Apparently she's sheltered many people before. Anyway,

I took the money we had saved toward our marriage and came down here."

"Why volunteer to work at the museum though? We don't have any connection with the labor unions—or with sheltering fugitives. It's only coincidence that Jesse's grandmother—"

"I know that, but Tomas is an artist; you've seen his style; it's very distinctive. And his paintings had started to sell in the past year; that's where what little money we had saved came from. I thought if he were hiding in a secure place he might try to paint, to raise money to send for Tommy and me. So the museum seemed a good place to be. Someone might hear of a new Chicano artist working in the area."

"It was certainly a long shot."

"Yes, but I was desperate. And it worked." She looked at Tomas Dominguez, her face softening.

"Was that what you planned to do?" I asked. "Sell the paintings and send for Emily and Tommy?"

"Yes." he said, looking me full in the eye. "Abuela Felicia suggested I paint. She intended to sell her own paintings, and she thought mine would attract less attention if grouped with hers than if I tried to sell them independently."

"And then what did you plan to do?"

"Take my family back to Mexico. I still do."

"Even though, as you claim, you aren't guilty of the murder?"

"I'm not guilty."

"Then why not fight the charges?"

"I wouldn't stand a chance."

"You don't know that. From what you've told me, they've got a circumstantial case at best."

"Elena," Emily said, "it's too much of a risk."

"I don't notice that you're one who avoids risks."

"I won't take a chance with Tomas's life."

It angered me—her willingness to sacrifice all three of

them, and his willingness to accept that sacrifice. "As it is,"
I said, "you're taking a chance with all three of your lives."

"How do you mean?" Tomas asked.

"If you go back to Mexico, you'll be a fugitive all your
life. And that will make Emily and Tommy fugitives too.
Emily will never see her family again. Tommy will never
know his maternal grandparents—people who, by Emily's
account, are good and would stand behind you as they did
behind her when she had the child."

They were both silent. I took advantage of it and pressed
on, at the same time wondering why I was arguing so fervently.
"Do you know what it's like in Mexico these days, Tomas?"

"I was born there."

"When did you come to the States?"

"Ten years ago."

"Then you probably don't remember what it's like. Mexico
is still a poor country; things have changed there, but not all
that much, and in some places not for the better. The life
down there isn't for people like you and Emily, especially the
life of a fugitive."

He seemed to think about it, then said flatly, "So what are
you going to do? Turn me in?"

"No, of course not. I'm not a cop, and I'm not here to
make moral or legal judgments."

"Why all this talk then?"

It was my turn to think. Why indeed? Because I liked
Emily; I thought she and her son deserved a better future than
the one Tomas was planning for them. And though I hardly
knew Tomas, I'd seen his work. That work alone made him
a worthwhile person. "Because what you're planning is stupid.
And because I hate to see someone destroy his own life and
the lives of those he loves by refusing to do what he knows
is right." The words sounded stuffy, and I wished we were
speaking in Spanish. They would still have sounded overly

pompous, but that gentle language would also have lent them a touch of poetry.

Tomas shrugged and looked at his hands. I stood up.

"I'm not going to preach at you anymore," I said. "And I'll still buy the paintings because, no matter what you decide to do, you'll need the money."

"Thank you," Emily said. "The painting I took is in the cottage. Abuela Felicia will give it to you. And don't worry about the car; I'll return it first thing in the morning."

"I'll call your landlady and let her know."

Then I turned and went outside. The clouds hung even lower over the hills now, and the air was muggy. Earthquake weather, Mama always called it—in spite of the fact that no quake ever materialized in response to her predictions.

Abuela Felicia was crossing toward the barn, reheated baby bottle in hand. I went up to her and said, "I need to talk to you."

She looked at the barn. "But the baby—"

"He can wait; he's not fussing." Taking her arm, I steered her back toward the cottage.

The painting Emily had taken was propped on the mantel. The old woman went straight to it and brought it to me, then gestured toward the couch. I sat down, leaning the painting against the coffee table, while she made herself comfortable in the platform rocker.

"Did you reach an agreement with them?" she asked in Spanish, motioning in the direction of the barn.

"If you mean, did I promise not to call the police, yes. Tomas says he's innocent, and it's none of my business anyway. But I think this idea of running to Mexico is foolish, and I told them so."

"I have told them that too. Perhaps hearing it from one of their own generation will make them change their minds."

"Perhaps."

"You saw the likeness to the story of Alberto Ortega?"

"Yes. And knowing what I know now, I wonder if Ortega would have survived if he hadn't run."

The old woman leaned forward, her eyes sharp with interest. "How do you mean?"

"If Ortega hadn't run to a lonely place, he wouldn't have been vulnerable. His killer would have had a far more difficult time of it."

"You say 'his killer' as if you knew who did it."

"I do." I went on to recount the true story of the slain soldiers.

When I was finished, Abuela Felicia was silent for a long time. "Of course," she finally said, "there are those who have suspected this. I, for one. But the proof—it rather destroys the legend, doesn't it?"

"Yes."

"And could do incalculable damage to our people's already shaky morale."

"Possibly, if the story ever came out."

She shrugged. "Why wouldn't it? One man was able to discover it. Others will. Besides, another murder has been committed—that of your friend, the professor." She sat back, folding her hands in her lap. "It is strange, isn't it, how the damage we do can wreak further damage down through the years?"

"Strange—and sad."

"Beatriz Garcia not only killed a good man, one who would have been of service to our people, but also killed two of his friends, merely because they happened to be there. And, indirectly, she killed an innocent woman—Victoria Piazza—because she couldn't face life without Ortega. Did I tell you this ranch is the original Piazza home?"

"No."

"I came to work for the family shortly after the great strike failed and my husband and I lost our livelihood. They allowed us all to live here, and they gave my husband work in the vineyards. I worked in the house and came to know Victoria well. She was a sad little thing, a woman lost."

I couldn't reply to that. A love like Victoria's for Ortega was something I doubted I'd ever experience.

Abuela Felicia said, "You say you think this professor was murdered because he had found out the true story of the slain soldiers?"

"Was about to find out."

"And do you now know who killed him?"

"I have my suspicions. It's possible Beatriz Garcia is still alive. She would be in her seventies. I've even toyed with the idea she might be living at my mother's trailer park in Goleta, Leisure Village. But, I don't know, it's such a remote possibility."

Abuela Felicia looked thoughtful but didn't comment.

"Or it could be someone from the labor movement who didn't want the legend exposed for what it was."

"No!"

I was surprised at the vehemence of her response. "You don't think they're capable of it? That exposure could damage their cause when it is fragile at best."

She hesitated. "I suppose I don't want to think any of our people capable of that."

"I understand. Abuela Felicia, there's one thing that bothers me about Ortega's death—the medallion that was ripped from his body. You mentioned it, remember?"

"Yes."

"Why would Beatriz take it?"

"It was a symbol of the struggle. But, more important, it was a gift from Beatriz. Interesting, too, that it had originally been a gift *to* Beatriz, from a former lover, a Hopi Indian whom she had known in Colorado when she and her father were organizing the grape pickers there. Apparently, Beatriz had no scruples about giving it away."

"Nor Ortega about wearing it."

She nodded reluctantly. "He was not a completely scrupulous man, but I have to believe that he would have changed. After all, he was still a young man; had he made his intended marriage, it might have transformed him."

"Maybe." But I was doubtful. I'd never ascribed to the theory of miraculous change after marriage. "Let me ask you this: Did Beatriz Garcia ever practice judo?"

"Judo? She had knowledge of self-defense, that I know. Whether it was judo or some other discipline, I can't be sure. But it was rough on the picket lines, and Beatriz was always one to take care of herself. She was a woman strong in body as well as in mind."

"And this medallion—what did it look like?"

"It was a grape cluster of hammered silver, to symbolize the struggle Beatriz and her lover had been through in Colorado. He was a craftsman, I believe, and made it specially for her."

I nodded, then reached for the painting and my bag. "You are still planning to buy the paintings?" Abuela Felicia asked.

"Of course. Once this Fiesta nonsense is over, the museum will be quieter, and then I can appraise them. I'll take it to the board and have a figure for you by next week."

"Fiesta?" she asked vaguely, and I knew she was thinking of the Fiesta of the Slain Soldiers.

"Fiesta week, in Santa Barbara. There have been great numbers of tourists, and someone at the museum got the idea we must have a float."

"Ah, I remember now. There is a parade tonight."

"And parties and . . . oh, *por Dios!*" I looked at my watch. It was nearly seven.

"What is it, Elena?"

"I have a date tonight for one of those parties. And I don't think I'm going to make it on time." And I could not think of a worse man to stand up than the chairman of our board of directors.

Seventeen

On the drive to Santa Barbara, my thoughts skipped back and forth between Emily and Tomas's dilemma and my own problem about what to tell Carlos. He had planned to pick me up at seven, so by now he would have realized I'd stood him up. I wondered how he would react; Carlos had a hot temper and might go off into one of his short-lived but dramatic rages. On the other hand, he might also pretend cool indifference in order to save face. I was hoping for the latter.

As the road approached the coast, the clouds disappeared and evening sunlight dappled the fields. I tried to dismiss my disturbing thoughts by enjoying the scenery: vineyards and orchards, as well as several acres of what I thought at first were brilliant yellow flowers. When I came closer to them, however, I realized that what I had taken for blossoms were really crookneck squash hanging heavy on their vines. Funny, I thought. I knew what kinds of crops they grew on the farms along this road, and I also knew it was too late in the year for any of them to be flowering. But I'd still perceived the yellow splashes of color to be blossoms rather than fruit. The mind was an odd thing, in the way it could sometimes see what it wanted or expected to, rather than what really existed.

Funny . . .

And then I thought of something else. Remembered something else. And suddenly I knew who had killed Ciro and tried twice to murder me.

I pressed my foot down on the accelerator, urging Nick's old car to its top speed. I had to get to a phone booth in a hurry.

The first booth I found was at a gas station on the frontage road off Route 101. I pulled in and jumped from the car, fumbling for change. On my first try, the line for the sheriff's station was busy. When I got through, they said Dave Kirk was off duty. I dug in my bag for more change and the paper on which I'd written his home number. The phone there rang ten times before I gave up.

Where was he? It was Saturday; probably he had a date. The thought surprised me—not because I didn't expect him to have dates but because it brought forth a strong twinge of jealousy. Impatiently, I dismissed the feeling; I had more important things to consider now.

What to do? I had wanted Dave's opinion and help. I couldn't just blunder along on my own. But there was no time to explain the whole complicated story to someone else in the sheriff's department. Perhaps Dave was only away from home momentarily. If I called back in fifteen minutes . . .

And then I thought of the painting in the car. I should take it to the museum, where it would be safe. Much as I wanted to continue acting as a detective, I was cursed with the strange psychology of a born curator: the preservation of works of art, no matter how valuable, came before anything else. I would take the painting to the museum, then call Dave from there. If he still wasn't home, I'd have to go ahead all alone. I retrieved my dimes from the coin return and went back to the car.

The downtown area was more crowded than it had been all week. Some of the streets had been blocked off for tonight's parade, due to start within the hour. I hadn't been prepared for such congestion; in previous years the parade had been held in the afternoon, but for some reason, this year it had been shifted to the more prominent slot of Saturday night.

Naturally, the attendance—and accompanying confusion—was greater than I ever remembered it.

My frustration mounted as I came upon police barriers and patrolmen who were rerouting traffic. It took a full fifteen minutes to get from Route 101 to the museum, and when I did arrive, I couldn't go into the parking lot because its entrance was blocked by the float. Cursing, I drove down the block looking for a parking space. In my Rabbit, that would have posed less of a problem, but Nick's old Dodge required extra room. When I finally found a space large enough, I spent precious minutes tugging and hauling at the wheel to maneuver the car in.

Taking the painting, I jumped out and ran toward the museum parking lot. A crowd of people—Susana, Linda, Jesse, and several volunteers—were milling about, putting last-minute touches on the giant *camaleone*. I glanced at it, noting with relief that it looked as good as it had that afternoon, then started for the loading-dock door.

"Elena!" It was Susana's voice.

I turned. She wore a shocking pink dress and had her hair piled in an elaborate arrangement. Smiling, she motioned for me to come over. A gangly man with an unruly shock of blond hair and a rumpled tan suit stood beside her. Who? Her date, probably. What a time to introduce me to a date!

"Susana," I said, "I have to hurry and make a phone call."

"But first you must meet Andy Kern."

Andy Kern. The name was familiar. I gave him a distracted smile and said, "Hello. Susana, I'm sorry but—"

"Elena." There was a warning note in her voice. "This is *the* Andy Kern, from the *News-Press*. He is here to do a story on us."

Por Dios! Of course, he was one of the paper's star reporters. "I see. What kind of story?"

Kern glanced around. His disdain for the subject matter could not have been more apparent had he wrinkled his sharply pointed nose. "My editor wants me to get something ethnic, in honor of the conclusion of Fiesta week. Your museum is about as ethnic as I could come up with."

I glanced at Susana. Her smile was strained. I felt my own defenses rise. "Yes. Well. I guess we *are* ethnic, as you put it. We are also very busy, as you can see."

He looked around again, and this time the corners of his thin lips twitched derisively. "It will only take a few minutes."

"Perhaps sometime next week. Or even tomorrow—"

"We plan to run the story tomorrow."

"Oh. Well, I'm sure Ms. Ibarra can help you. She handles our public relations."

Susana blinked in astonishment.

"Ms. Ibarra said she has to leave with the float."

That damned float! "I'm sure she can stay a little longer. She can explain about the float and the artwork it is modeled on."

Susana opened her mouth to protest, but I silenced her with a glare.

Andy Kern was getting out a pad and pencil. "That sounds like the kind of thing I'm looking for." Then he glanced over at the float, no longer bothering to conceal his condescension. "After all, it's so—"

"I know," I said dryly. "So ethnic." Then I turned and went up the steps to the loading dock, muttering, "Supercilious Anglo prick!" I didn't bother to keep my voice down, and from the way Andy Kern's posture stiffened, I knew he'd heard me. I'd probably cost us a good story in the paper, but then, given the reporter's attitude, how good would it have been anyway?

Once inside, I went immediately to the basement and put Tomas Dominguez's painting with the others. After checking the temperature-and-humidity gauge, I hurried back upstairs to the office wing and tried Dave Kirk's number again. No answer. I'd have to go ahead on my own, as I'd decided earlier. I put down the receiver and went back outside to the parking lot, coming face to face with Jesse Herrera and Emily Hitchens.

"Emily," I said, "what are you doing here in town?"

"I came in to return my landlady's car."

"But then why did you come to the museum?"

She and Jesse glanced at each other. He said, "She came to find me because she's worried about Abuela Felicia."

"Why? Has something happened to her?"

"It's like this," Emily said. "Immediately after you left the ranch, she brought Tommy's bottle to the barn and asked me if I would drive her to Goleta, to a trailer park called Leisure Village. She said she had been invited to a party there. I was to return the car and wait to hear from her, and then she would have Jesse drive us back to Ojai. I didn't like to leave Tomas and Tommy, but it seemed a good solution to the problem of my landlady's car, so I said I would bring her."

"Wait," I said. "Leisure Village is my mother's trailer park."

"Oh. Well, she didn't say anything about knowing your mother. Just that she was going to a party. After I dropped her off there, though, I got worried about her. And when I got back here to Santa Barbara, I decided I'd better check with Jesse to make sure everything was all right."

"What started you worrying?"

"For one thing, she didn't know where the trailer park was; we had to stop and ask directions. If she had friends there, she would have known. And she didn't act as if she was going to a party—she was all tense and fidgety, yet sort of determined. I sensed she might even be angry."

I looked at Jesse. *"Does* your grandmother know anyone at the park?"

He spread his hands. "I doubt it. She hardly ever ventures off that ranch, hasn't for years."

I thought of Abuela Felicia's connection with Victoria Piazza and her devotion to the Chicano labor movement. How she must hate the woman whose crime had driven Victoria to her death, the woman whose crime had first perpetrated and now threatened to destroy one of the labor movement's greatest legends. Felicia had known Beatriz Garcia; even now she might recognize her, aged and changed as she was.

"Elena," Jesse said, "what's wrong?"

"I think your grandmother may be in danger."

"Why, what's going on?"

"I'll explain on the way to Leisure Village. You drive; your car is faster than the clunker I'm using."

He nodded and reached into the pocket of his jeans for his keys.

"What about me?" Emily called as we started across the parking lot. "What can I do?"

"Say here." I said. "We'll be in touch."

"Elena!" Susan was running after us, her high heels tapping on the pavement. "Jesse cannot leave. He must drive the float."

"Damn the float! Get someone else to drive."

"Elena!"

"I said get someone else. Get—" I looked around and saw Carlos Bautista coming through the crowd toward me. He must have decided to track me down and drag me off to that party. "Get Carlos to drive it."

"Carlos is chairman of the board of directors!"

"Yes, and chairmen are generally very smart people. He'll know what to do." And then I grabbed Jesse's arm and we started running for the street.

By the time we arrived at the trailer park, I'd told Jesse the full story of the slain soldiers and Ciro Sisnero's murder. He was definitely alarmed about Abuela Felecia's safety, but not so much that he wouldn't be of help to me. When he pulled his car up in front of the rec center, we got out unhurriedly so we wouldn't call undue attention to ourselves and approached the building.

The door to the office was closed, and the lounge was deserted, but on the patio about twenty people milled about, and I could smell burning charcoal from the barbecue pit. The piñatas I'd seen earlier in Nick's car had been hung from the lattice, and crepe-paper streamers decorated the supporting beams. A festive-looking table had been set up near the pool, uncomfortably close to the planter box where Ciro had hit his head and died, and in its center was a punch bowl surrounded by paper cups. I glanced around but didn't see anyone I was looking for.

This didn't seem like enough people for one of the park's big parties, and I wondered if Ciro's death had cast a pall that was keeping most of the residents away. Or had something else happened?

Then I saw Mama, coming through the door with a big pan of what had to be enchiladas in her asbestos-mittened hands. Jesse noticed her at the same time and went up and tried to take the pan from her. She motioned him away. "You will burn yourself. Let me do it." Setting the pan on the table, she turned and said, "What brings the two of you here?"

I ignored the question. "Where is everybody?"

"It is early yet. Most have taken the bus into Santa Barbara to see the parade."

"Who?"

Mama looked puzzled at the urgency of my question but said, "The usual crowd who don't have sense enough to stay home. Nick, Mary Jaramillo, Adela, the Walterses—"

"How long ago did they leave?"

She frowned. "Maybe half an hour. What is it, Elena?"

"Do you know where they were planning to view the parade from?"

"No, just somewhere along the route. But you could probably locate them by looking for where the bus is parked. It's the yellow school bus from the Goleta charter company that we always have."

"Mama, you should be a detective. Come on, Jesse." Then I stopped. "Wait—did you see an old lady here earlier? A little, stooped old lady with light gray hair? Wearing black, sort of old-fashioned clothes?"

She considered. "Yes, as a matter of fact, I did. She was getting on the bus, at the end of the line. I thought she must be someone's guest, since I didn't recognize her."

Jesse and I turned and ran toward his car.

"Elena!" Mama called. "What is going on?"

I didn't take time to answer her.

Eighteen

BY THE TIME we reached Santa Barbara, the parade had already left its staging area on Cabrillo Boulevard, on the beachfront at the foot of State Street. Police barricades were up everywhere, and beyond them I could see throngs of people wandering along the broad sidewalks. The air was filled with the sounds of children, police whistles, vendors hawking ice cream and soda pop. An occasional firecracker went off, causing both Jesse and me to start.

Jesse tugged the wheel of his car viciously as we went around corner after corner, looking for the yellow bus and a place to park. The parking situation was hopeless, however: All nine lots that offered free ninety-minute parking were full, and cars were bumper to bumper along the curbs. After a while I realized that even if we did find the bus, it wouldn't be much help in locating where its passengers were viewing the parade; with all this congestion, the city would certainly have assigned special areas for bus parking.

Finally, I said to Jesse, "The only way we're going to locate them is on foot."

"So what am I to do? Abandon the car in the middle of the street?" His face was dark with frustration and anxiety.

"Of course not. What you should do is let me off right now. Then take the car to the museum; the float will be gone, and you'll be able to get into the lot."

"You forget there's a security chain across the lot at night."

"Ah, but you are speaking to the director. I have a key." I dug it from my purse and handed it to him, then indicated that he should leave me at the corner of Ortega Street. The museum was several blocks away, in an area of historic buildings that had been restored, and in this traffic it would take him some time to get there.

"How will I know where to find you?" he asked.

"You won't. From here on out, we'll work on our own." Before he could protest, I got out of the car and began hurrying to the right, toward State Street and the central part of the parade route.

The procession hadn't gotten this far—it was probably still wending its way along Cabrillo, past the official reviewing stand and box seats. The sidewalks of State were jammed, and people pushed their way in and out of the expensive stores, which were still open, softly lit against the encroaching darkness. The restaurants and bars were mobbed, and other people sat on the curbs or the planter boxes and benches, eating ice cream and popcorn and the wonderful avocado halves filled with salsa from El Mercado. Many of them wore the green and purple plastic phosphorescent necklaces sold by one of the service clubs; their strands were so bright that they made the wearers' faces glow eerily in the dark. I walked along quickly, glancing from side to side for someone I recognized.

The streets were filled with tourists toting their inevitable guidebooks and cameras. Young parents who struggled to keep their numerous charges together. Teenagers who held hands and otherwise fondled one another as they ambled along the sidewalk. Other teenagers who smiled vacuously and swayed to the music from their Sony Walkmans. Upscale chic types who seemed to have invaded the area in droves during the past few years. Children running amok. Children waiting patiently for the parade. Older people looking with disapproval upon the rowdier revelers. Older people smiling tolerantly. Older people who *were* rowdy revelers. But no older people who resembled the group from Leisure Village.

I made my way down the sidewalk, dodging clumps of bystanders and moving bicycles. The air was warm and moist from the sea, and I could smell the blossoms of the flame trees and the heavier odors of popcorn and tacos. I bumped into people, jostled others, almost tripped over a child on a skateboard. I apologized absently, my eyes moving over the thick crowd. Where were the people from the trailer park? Where would they have chosen to view the parade?

In the distance, I could hear the sound of music. Not the blasting, patriotic tunes usually played by brass bands in a parade, but gentler, lilting Spanish melodies. I pushed to the curb—again apologizing—and leaned forward, catching a view of the banners that led the procession far down near the intersection of Haley and State. I swept my gaze down the front rows of onlookers as far as I could see. No one.

Stepping back, with yet more apologies, I stood still and considered. Chances were, the group from the trailer park would not have wanted to plunge into the thick of the rowdy crowd. They were more likely to be up at the far end of State, near the parade route's end at Sola, where the sidewalks would be less packed. I turned and began to work my way north, past City Hall and Plaza de la Guerra, where El Mercado was set up. Its stalls were doing a brisk business; the spicy scent of food drifted out, causing me to feel a sharp pang of hunger.

I hurried past the Santa Barbara Art Museum—an airy-looking modern building that presented a not-unpleasant contrast to the white stucco, tile-roofed structures that were standard under the city's building code. Beyond that, in the final two blocks of the parade route, the crowds were thinner.

But the people I sought weren't among them, either. I paused at Sola, then ran across State and started down the opposite sidewalk. The sound of the bands was louder now as the parade approached, and near the corner of Figueroa I came to a complete standstill, trapped with hundreds of other stationary people. I moved to the left and the right, tried squirming and using my elbows, but nothing worked. I now understood the concept of gridlock.

Over the heads and between the shoulders of the people around me, I could see the color guard that led the parade. Next came the high-stepping band, playing an old Spanish tune that was vaguely familiar. A white Cadillac convertible bore the mayor, followed by cars full of other dignitaries. And then came the *caballeros* on horseback, their mounts prancing smartly. *Vaqueros* in chaps and fancy jackets and silver spurs twirled their *reatas* at the crowd, causing gasps as the ropes snapped above the heads of those in the front rows. Señoritas in rainbow-hued satins trimmed with lace waved and smiled from flower-decked floats. There were more bands, mariachis, more prancing horses. Finally I spied the museum's great crepe-paper *camaleone*.

In spite of my anxiety about Abuela Felicia, I couldn't help but admire the job our people had done. The dragon's head rose high, vicious fangs exposed, brilliant red tongue seeming to flicker. The bird-body was gracefully shaped, its wings soaring aloft. It was almost as if life had been breathed into Jesse's smaller papier-mâché creation, and I hoped he had parked the car and gotten back here in time to see it in motion. Murmurs of appreciation rose from the crowd, and I felt a surge of pride. The float was good, very good, and Susana deserved most of the credit. I'd been negative and discouraging about the project—and even more negative about Susana—while she, with the spirit of enthusiasm and fun that belongs naturally to those of seventeen, had gone ahead and gotten the job done. She deserved a raise, possibly even a promotion for this. So what if she was ambitious? If I put that ambition to good use, she would be no threat to me, and we had needed a permanent public-relations person for a long time—

And then I spied Nick. He was leaning against a planter box next to one of his runner friends, pointing to the *camaleone* and smiling. I began working with my elbows again, and after a major effort I managed to reach them. Nick turned to me, his face alight with childlike pleasure.

"Elena," he said, "it's a masterpiece! Gabriela will be sorry she missed this. You must have pictures taken—"

"Nick, where are the others?"

He stopped, surprised.

"The others who came on the bus—where are they?"

"Oh, around." He shrugged. "This kind of crowd, we got separated. Most of them wanted to stay down near the staging area where the bus parking is. Didn't want to walk so far. But my buddy and me, we're runners, got stamina. Wanted to go where the excitement was."

"The bus is down on Cabrillo?"

"In the beach parking, yes."

But that didn't really help me. I was fairly sure Abuela Felicia wouldn't be returning to the bus. "Did you see an unfamiliar woman on the bus?" I asked. "Very old-looking, stooped, wearing all black?"

"Yeah. Who is she? She looked old enough to be my mother."

"Who was she with?"

"Nobody, as far as I could tell."

"Did you see where she went when she got off?"

"No, not as I recall."

"Thanks, Nick." The people were moving once again, now that the parade had passed. I started down the sidewalk, toward the beach. Nick called something after me, but I didn't hear what it was.

The crowd was thinning rapidly, but despite the short respite caused by my pleasure over the museum's float, I felt my irritation increasing. I speeded up to a half-run, bumping into

children, pushing past adults, with no apologies now. I ha
to find them, had to stop what was a potential tragedy.

And then I saw a familiar stooped figure crossing Stat
Street. Abuela Felicia was walking haltingly but with stead
determination. I called out to her, but she didn't turn her head
She stepped onto the opposite curb and vanished behind
TV camera crew that was packing up there. I ran acros
nearly crashed into a newscaster whose face was famili a
from the eleven o'clock broadcasts, and looked around fo
the old woman.

She was moving down Canon Perdido, through the throng
that converged on Plaza de la Guerra for this final night c
dancing and festivities at El Mercado. I went after her, agai
employing my body-blocking tactics. People stepped aside t
let her pass; after all, she was old and looked fragile. I, o
the other hand, got no preferential treatment, and in spite c
my ability to walk faster, I began to lose ground. I dodge
and weaved, trying to keep Felicia in sight. She continue
along the sidewalk, past the plaza, and turned left into th
shadows on Anacapa Street.

I quickened my pace until I was free of the crowd onc
more, but when I rounded the corner I found I could no longe
see her. In her black outfit, she might be very near, movin
in the darkness created by the trees and shrubs. I stopped t
take my bearings.

Two blocks ahead was the county courthouse—a large
graceful structure with wrought-iron balconies, mosaics,
red-tiled roof, and a tower. Set on a square block of beautiful
landscaped lawns and sunken gardens, it loomed starkly whit
in the glare of floodlights. The tower—called El Mirador—
was a tall sentinel against the cloud-dusted sky. In spite c
the commotion only a block away, the courthouse and i
grounds seemed quiet and serene.

I studied them, wondering if Jesse's grandmother could b
going there, and decided it was unlikely. Just as I was abou

o turn and look the other way, however, I spied her, walking aster now down the opposite side of Anacapa Street near the courthouse entrance. Crossing the street myself, I debated alling out to her, then decided to follow in silence.

Felicia made no attempt to enter the building, which by now was closed to visitors. Instead, she continued along the block to Anapamu Street and turned right. Once she disappeared, I started to run, slowing down only when I got to the corner. Abuela Felicia had vanished into the shadows once more. I hurried around the building just in time to see her going down the stone steps to the sunken garden. Halfway across the lawn, I thought I saw another figure—taller and more vigorous-looking—moving ahead of us. In what little light filtered through the trees, I couldn't tell if the other person was male or female.

I paused, watching Felicia walk carefully down the steps and start across the lawn. The other person had disappeared down a path that wound past a bed of birds of paradise. The long stalks and oddly shaped flowers stood out pale against the darker vegetation, but otherwise I could see nothing. The grounds were quiet, eerily quiet now, and I had a sudden feeling of urgency. I must overtake her without frightening her.

I went down the steps quickly and moved across the lawn. Felicia was silhouetted against the pale flowers for an instant, and then she was gone. Cursing my prior hesitation, I ran across the rest of the lawn and down the little path.

The path curved off under the thick branches of a bottlebrush tree. The soft red blossoms hung so low that they brushed my cheek as I passed. I could smell jasmine and other flowers, as well as the dank odor of freshly turned earth. From the distance came the sound of automobile horns and music at El Mercado, but here in the darkness all was silent. I stopped, straining to see into the tangle of trees ahead of me.

Someone touched my arm.

I jumped, stifling a cry, and turned to face Abuela Felici▪ Her face was a pale oval above the black of her clothing, a▪ she put a finger to her lips. Then she pointed down the pa▪ toward the thick shrubbery. Her mouth moved and I leane▪ closer.

She whispered, almost inaudibly, "It's her."

"Beatriz." I kept my voice low too.

"Yes."

"Stay here."

I started forward, peering into the darkness around me. T▪ path seemed to end a few feet away. The border of vegetatio▪ could not be more than a couple of yards thick before ▪ stopped at the sidewalk of the street beyond. Beatriz cou▪ have gone through there and simply walked away. But the▪ why had she led Felicia here in the first place?

Suddenly I realized how foolish it was to follow her int▪ this dark, isolated place. Foolish and unnecessary. Abue▪ Felicia had seen the woman and identified her. She cou▪ identify her once again—to the sheriff's men. The importa▪ thing was to get Jesse's grandmother away from here and int▪ protective custody before—

There was a sudden movement behind me. Strong arm▪ encircled my neck, wrenching me backward. I clawed at th▪ arms, but they closed tighter, shutting off air from my win▪ pipe. I gasped, clawed harder, kicked out desperately wit▪ my feet. My assailant dragged me back farther, slamming m▪ into a tree trunk as we went.

My knees gave out, and the pressure on my throat increase▪ as my body sagged. I tried to suck in air, but none woul▪ come. I could feel myself starting to lose consciousness.

Something struck both of us with a sudden impact; I hea▪ a grunt from my attacker. The arms around my throat let g▪ I fell to the ground, gulping in great lungfuls of air, my ea▪ ringing.

Shaking my head, I lifted myself up onto one knee. The▪

vere gruntings and thrashings in the shrubbery to my right.
Two people were locked together, swaying this way and that
n a violent embrace.

I braced my palms against the ground and pushed to my
feet. Dizzily, I lurched forward. The taller figure shoved the
other away, and there was a snapping noise as if something
had ripped or broken. The taller woman rushed at me, but I
sidestepped, and she stumbled and fell. I threw myself on her,
pummeling her with my fists . . . then realized that the body
beneath me lay inert.

I got up and staggered over to where the other woman lay
supine. Abuela Felicia, her head resting against the roots of
a bottlebrush tree. She was breathing hard, but her eyes were
wide open, gleaning fiercely in what little light penetrated the
overhead branches. She held her hand out to me.

At first I thought she wanted me to help her up, but then
saw the silver chain dangling from her fist. "Take it," she
said in a gasping voice.

I knelt and reached for it. Attached to the broken chain was
a silver medallion—a grape cluster. The same medallion that
Beatriz Garcia had ripped from Alberto Ortega's dead body
some forty-eight years before.

The same medallion I'd seen in Adela Hernandez's apartment some four days before. Only then I'd taken it to be
silver squash blossoms.

It was funny, the way the mind saw what it expected to,
rather than what was. . . .

Nineteen

AT ELEVEN O'CLOCK on Sunday morning, I was lounging b
the pool at Leisure Village, surrounded by a rapt group c
people, none of whom was under sixty-five. A few yard
away, but within earshot, my mother was cleaning up th
remnants of the previous evening's party, aided by Nick and—
of all people—Dave Kirk. My policeman friend had been
source of pleasant surprise to me all morning.

After I'd given him a formal statement wrapping up th
last details of the case against Adela Hernandez, Dave ha
suggested he follow me to the trailer park so I could retur
Nick's car. Then, he added, we could go on a picnic if I liked
He knew a nice beach a little farther north that was seldor
crowded. Pleased by the invitation, I had agreed.

But when we'd arrived at the park, we'd been cornered b
at least a dozen residents, including Mama and Nick. The
had wanted to know exactly what had happened with Adel
and why. And they had wanted to hear it from me, the perso
who'd solved the case, rather than from Dave, who was merel
an official. Dave had seemed unperturbed by this, and he'
been so helpful to Mama that by now I was certain she ha
forgiven him for being an Anglo. The other people aroun
the pool had accepted him without question. Just another c
Elena's boyfriends, their manner seemed to say, and a mor
presentable one than most.

All in all, his behavior that morning—coupled with th

ct he'd been doing his laundry when I'd tried to call him
e night before—was making him seem like a very good
atch. I still had my reservations about becoming involved
ith him; I wasn't at all sure I ever wanted another relationship
ith an Anglo. None of my previous relationships with Anglos
ad turned out well. But, I reminded myself, a date for a
icnic does not constitute a proposal of marriage. I would go
owly, wait and see. And enjoy myself in the meantime.

But before we could go on that picnic, I had to sit down
nd explain everything. I had told the real story of the slain
oldiers to the little group and reconstructed how Adela Her-
andez—née Beatriz Adela Garcia—had fled to Los Angeles.
a her partial confession from her hospital bed—where she
as being treated for a broken arm and slight concussion—
he had stated that she had worked as a domestic there for a
w years and eventually married. She and her husband had
perated the souvenir shop she'd spoken of on Olvera Street
r upward of thirty years, but after his death she had retired
» Santa Barbara and the job as manager of the trailer park.
he had been confident her true identity would never come
» light after all those years, and it probably would not have
it hadn't been for Ciro.

Now Mary Jaramillo said, "I still don't understand how
dela found out what Ciro was researching. The woman is
emiliterate; surely she couldn't have seen his ad in the histori-
al journal." Mary's raised eyebrows and flaring nostrils told
s all what she thought of the poorly educated who had made
o attempt to better themselves. Stretched out on her lounge
hair, her limbs splayed indolently, she resembled her haughty
at, the British colonel.

"She didn't see the ad," I said. "She found out the same
ay she learned I was going to the historical society in Bakers-
eld. And I'm afraid she found out from you, Mary."

"What? From *me?*"

"You read the journal regularly. You saw the ad, did you?"

"Well, of course I did. And I asked Ciro about it. It was strange way to be doing scholarly research, putting an ad there like it was some sort of personals column for the lovlorn—"

"Where were you when you asked him?"

"Here at the pool."

"The same place my mother was when she talked abo my trip to Bakersfield."

"But—"

"Adela was manager here. She was always around, but s went unnoticed. It's like the butler in mystery novels—h in a perfect position to find out a great deal, because h only a servant and people simply don't think about hir Adela overheard your conversation with Ciro about his and became afraid of what he might find out. So she tel phoned him, disguising her voice, and told him not to contin his research. When that didn't work, she waited until almo everyone was at El Mercado last Monday, started talking him about judo, got him in a hold, and killed him. Or so v assume; she hasn't admitted it yet."

"And she was also the person who blew up Ciro's trail and tried to run you off the road on the way back fro Bakersfield?" Mama asked, with an angry, protective glea in her eyes.

Dave said to her, "The paint scrapes and dents on Adel car are pretty clear evidence of that—although she's n admitting anything on that score, or confessing she broke in the trailer and stole documents from his ffiles."

"Why on earth not?" Nick asked. "She's already confess to three murders."

Dave dumped a pile of dirty paper plates into a green plast trash bag. "In her mind she seems to have separated Beatr Garcia from Adela Hernandez. When she talked about t slain soldiers, it was as if someone else had committed the murders. But attempted murder on Elena—twice—and later on Jesse Herrera's grandmother—well, she can't face the fact that Adela Hernandez would do such things."

Mama nodded, anger replaced by understanding. "After all, it's been a long time since she *was* Beatriz Garcia."

"There's no statute of limitations on murder," Dave said.

"Surely, at her age—"

"Yes, at her age she'll receive a light sentence." Dave looked disapproving, and—remembering her strong arms trying to choke the life out of me—I had to concur. I had liked Adela; she could be crusty, but there was something steely and uncompromising there that I'd had to admire. But I could not forget Alberto Ortega, his two compadres, and Victoria Piazza. To say nothing of Ciro, and the terror I'd felt, not once but three times, at her hands.

"Speaking of Jesse's grandmother," Nick said, "is she okay?"

"Yes, she's a surprisingly tough woman," I replied. "They released her from the hospital emergency room last night after treating her for cuts and bruises. At her insistence, Jesse took her and Emily, the woman who drove her here, back to Ojai."

Mama turned to Dave and said, "Come sit awhile. You've helped enough."

He followed her over to our little group, where they took chairs on the periphery. Nick—who had not been similarly relieved of his housekeeping duties—made a sound that was somewhere between a sniff and a snort, and sat down too.

Gloria Walters asked me, "Just what did the old lady think she was doing anyway?"

I smiled, thinking that Gloria and Felicia were almost the same age. "Being a detective. She hated Beatriz Garcia and was sure she could identify her."

"And the girl who drove her here?" Sam asked. "Wasn't she a museum employee?"

"An, that's an interesting tale." I explained about Emily and Tomas Dominguez. "Jesse called me this morning and said Tomas has decided to return to Visalia and stand trial. Emily will remain here for a while and try to earn money— both for the costs of his defense and the family's support."

"How?" Mary asked.

"Oh, there are ways," I said, thinking about my plan for promoting Susana and hiring Emily as my secretary—not to mention arranging for a proper outlet for Tomas Dominguez's work through a gallery owner I knew.

"Back to Adela," Mama said, "did you know she was the murderer when you went after Felicia?"

"I was pretty sure. I'd never suspected Adela before, because she'd kept in such good shape and looks much younger than seventy-four. I took her to be in her sixties." Turning to look at Dave, I added, "Adela, it turns out, practiced judo and swam daily. We could have found that out by asking any number of the residents. When I got the list of people who had attended Ciro's classes from her, it never occurred to me that she had simply left herself off."

"I made the same mistake," he said.

"But how did you figure out it was her?" Mama asked me.

"I'd seen the grape-cluster medallion. Apparently she wore it frequently, but on the morning I first noticed it, she'd been cleaning it, along with some silverware and a tea set, and it was lying on a table in her apartment. I didn't pay much attention to it, though, and took it to be squash blossoms, like a lot of Indian silver necklaces are."

"And?"

"And then Abuela Felicia told me about the medallion that had been ripped from Alberto Ortega's body. It was a grape cluster. That still didn't mean anything to me until I was driving back from Ojai and mistook a field of crookneck squash for yellow flowers. That got me to thinking about how we sometimes see what we expect to see rather than what's actually there, and I guess I made some sort of mental leap from squash to squash blossoms."

"The intuitive and creative side of detective work," Dave said.

I glanced at him to see if he was being sarcastic, but his smile told me otherwise.

The elderly people who were gathered around me fell silent now, each deep in thought. Probably, I guessed, they were reviewing their own lives, thinking of times when each of them could have gone as wrong as Adela had. I knew, because I'd had similar thoughts in the early hours of the morning, and I had had far fewer opportunities than any of them.

"Say," Sam Walters said abruptly, "where does Joe Garcia fit into this? Why did he up and disappear?"

Dave said, "Garcia—no relation to Beatriz—had a record. I found that out when I ran a check on him. And, according to his girlfriend at the Low-Ball Bar, he was also dealing marijuana. When he started seeing a lot of police around here after Ciro's death, he got edgy and took off." As he finished speaking, Dave made a swift motion with his head, meaning it was time to leave for our picnic.

I stood up. "That about covers everything."

"No," Mama said, "it doesn't."

"What else is there?"

"Your date with Carlos Bautista."

Carlos! Once again I had forgotten him. "Where did you hear about that?"

She and Nick exchanged glances. "He called yesterday evening, looking for you."

"I take it you stood him up."

"Well. . ."

Mama's eyes twinkled and she glanced at Dave. "A fine man like that, stood up on Fiesta weekend."

"I . . ." I stopped. Dave was watching me intently, and he looked more than a little bit jealous.

"And he's your boss, too," Mary said, obviously relishing my discomfort. "You could lose that fancy job."

"I don't think Elena has anything to worry about," Nick said.

We all turned toward him.

"I ran into Carlos last night near where the parade ended."

"Oh?" I said.

"He was having a terrific time. Said he'd really enjoyed driving the museum float, had had more fun than if he'd gone to a hundred society parties." Nick paused, grinning slyly at me. "In fact, he was heading off to a party right then—with a pretty young lady in a pink dress, name of Susana. I guess, like the rest of us old fogeys, he's learning to live a little."

Strange, but it didn't bother me in the slightest. I held out my hand to Dave and said, "Good for him. And now, if you'll excuse us, *we* are going to head off on a picnic."

Nick shook his white head. "Why don't you two live it up yourselves? Go sailboating. Waterskiing. How about sky-diving?"

"No, thanks," I said as Dave and I walked hand in hand toward the parking lot. "I'll stick to more sedentary activities—until I'm at least sixty."

Welcome to the Island of Morada—getting there is easy, leaving . . . is murder.

Embark on the ultimate, on-line, fantasy vacation with
MODUS OPERANDI.

Join fellow mystery lovers in the murderously fun MODUS OPERANDI, a unique on-line, multi-player, multi-service, interactive, mystery game launched by The Mysterious Press, Time Warner Electronic Publishing and Simutronics Corporation.

Featuring never-ending foul play by your favorite Mysterious Press authors and editors, MODUS OPERANDI is set on the fictional Caribbean island of Morada. Forget packing, passports and planes, entry to Morada is easy—all you need is a vivid imagination.

Simutronics GameMasters are available in MODUS OPERANDI around the clock, adding new mysteries and puzzles, offering helpful hints, and taking you virtually by the hand through the killer gaming environment as you come in contact with players from on-line services the world over. Mysterious Press writers and editors will also be there to participate in real-time on-line special events or just to throw a few back with you at the pub.

MODUS OPERANDI is available on-line now.

Join the mystery and mayhem on:
- America Online® at keyword MODUS
- GEnie® on page 1615
- PRODIGY® at jumpword MODUS

Or call toll-free for sign-up information:
- America Online® 1 (800) 768-5577
- GEnie® 1 (800) 638-9636, use offer code DAF524
- PRODIGY® 1 (800) PRODIGY

Or take a tour on the Internet at
http://www. pathfinder.com/twep/games/modop.

MODUS OPERANDI—It's to die for.

©1995 Time Warner Electronic Publishing
A Time Warner Company

DON'T MISS ANY OF THESE RIVETING MYSTERIES STARRING PRIVATE EYE SHARON McCONE!

"Muller remains the best."—*San Diego Union-Tribune*

- *ASK THE CARDS A QUESTION*
  (0-445-40-849-9, $5.99 USA) ($6.99 CAN)
- *THE CHESHIRE CAT'S EYE*
  (0-445-40-850-2, $5.50 USA) ($6.99 CAN)
- *DOUBLE* with Bill Pronzini
  (0-446-40-413-6, $5.50 USA) ($6.99 CAN)
- *EDWIN OF THE IRON SHOES*
  (0-445-40-902-9, $5.99 USA) ($6.99 CAN)
- *EYE OF THE STORM*
  (0-445-40-625-9, $5.50 USA) ($6.99 CAN)
- *GAMES TO KEEP THE DARK AWAY*
  (0-445-40-851-0, $5.50 USA) ($6.99 CAN)
- *LEAVE A MESSAGE FOR WILLIE*
  (0-445-40-900-2, $5.50 USA) ($6.99 CAN)
- *PENNIES ON A DEAD WOMAN'S EYES*
  (0-446-40-033-5, $5.99 USA) ($6.99 CAN)
- *THE SHAPE OF DREAD*
  (0-445-40-916-9, $5.99 USA) ($6.99 CAN)
- *THERE'S NOTHING TO BE AFRAID OF*
  (0-445-40-901-0, $5.50 USA) ($6.99 CAN)
- *THERE'S SOMETHING IN A SUNDAY*
  (0-445-40-865-0, $5.99 USA) ($6.99 CAN)
- *TILL THE BUTCHERS CUT HIM DOWN*
  (0-446-60-302-3, $5.99 USA) ($6.99 CAN)
- *TROPHIES AND DEAD THINGS*
  (0-446-40-039-4, $5.99 USA) ($6.99 CAN)
- *WHERE ECHOES LIVE*
  (0-446-40-161-7, $5.99 USA) ($6.99 CAN)
- *WOLF IN THE SHADOWS*
  (0-445-40-383-0, $5.50 USA) ($6.99 CAN)

W

AVAILABLE AT A BOOKSTORE NEAR YOU FROM WARNER BOOKS

614-C